Tokaido Road

ナンシー・ガフィールド Nancy Gaffield
池田久代訳 Hisayo Ikeda

翻訳詩集
広重の「東海道五十三次之内」

A Poetic Response to the Print Series
Fifty-Three Stations of the Tokaido by Hiroshige Utagawa

First published in 2011
by CB editions
146 Percy Road London W12 9QL
www.cbeditions.com

All rights reserved
© Nancy Gaffield, 2011

The right of Nancy Gaffield to be identified as author
of this work has been asserted in accordance
with the Copyright, Designs and Patents Act 1988

Printed in England by Blissetts, London W3 8DH

ISBN 978–0–9567359–0–4

は じ め に

　この翻訳詩集『東海道ロード』を出版できることを本当にうれしく思います。日本を代表する浮世絵師である歌川広重の版画「東海道五拾三次之内」に思いを寄せて書かれたナンシー・ガフィールド博士の詩集 *Tokaido Road* に出会ってから数年、ようやくその詩集を、版画とともに日英両言語で、さらにガフィールド博士による詩の朗読と邦楽の音色を聴きながら鑑賞できるものとして完成しました。

　本書は、皇學館大学の日英比較文化研究会(Japan-UK Comparative Culture Workshop=JUCCW)が企画し編集したものです。皇學館大学とナンシー・ガフィールド博士が所属されている英国ケント大学とは2011年（平成23年）に教育および学術研究に関する協定を結び、学生は毎年夏季短期語学研修に参加しています。協定締結の際には、ガフィールド博士はダーウィン・カレッジの学寮長を務められており、とても尽力していただきました。ちょうどその年、博士の詩集 *Tokaido Road* が出版され、翌年の2012年（平成24年）にアルデブラ・ファースト・コレクション賞を受賞されました。私たちは、まずそのタイトル名に魅かれました。日本人の馴染みのある東海道五拾三次の浮世絵を題材にした詩集と知れば、興味を持たざるを得ません。そこで、平成25年に二つの大学の国際学術交流事業の一環として、日英比較文化研究会を立ち上げ、詩集 *Tokaido Road* を基にして日本と英国の比較文化研究をすることにしました。本学のある伊勢市とケント大学のあるカンタベリー市は、それぞれ伊勢神宮とカンタベリー大聖堂（イギリス国教会総本山）のお膝元で、ともに「聖地」であるという共通点もあり、現在この研究会は、文化・文学のみならず、宗教や巡礼などテーマを広げて活動をしています。

　さて、研究会では、大学教員の他に、学生、市民の参加も得て、広重の図版を鑑賞し、その宿場や土地の歴史を調べ、ガフィールド博士の英詩をひとつずつ紐解いていきました。研究会が進むにつれ、日本の代表的な東海道の55枚の図版をこんなに熱心に見たことがなかったことに気づかされました。そして、宿場めぐりをしたり、浮世絵が所蔵されている美術館を訪れたり、講義を受けたりと、広重の浮世絵について学習を重ねました。詩を解釈するにあたっては、とても難しいものがありました。図版のどの部分が詩の中に取り入れられているのだろうか、宿場町のこの歴史を取り挙げているのだろうかと説明的に読みがちですが、詩は図版の解説ではありません。しかし同時に、二つを切り離すこともできません。詩の解釈ではメンバーが様々に議論をしました。こうした研究会を経て、今回この翻訳詩集に辿りつきました。詩の邦訳は全て池田久代によるものですが、研究会の成果を踏まえて池田氏の感性で綴られたものです。

　最後に、ガフィール博士に感謝の気持ちをお伝えしたいと思います。平成25年11月に皇學館大学にて *Tokaido Road* について、平成27年11月には *Tokaido Road* をもとにして作られたオペラについて講演をしていただき、またその折には、メンバーと親睦を深めていただき座談会では質問等にお答えいただきました。今回の出版に際しては、翻訳の許可と朗読を快諾していただきました。研究会と翻訳企画にずっと変わらない協力をしていただきましたことに感謝申し上げます。

　なお、この研究会の活動と本書の出版は皇學館大学の助成を受けています。暖かい支援にお礼を申し上げます。

日英比較文化研究会
児玉 玲子

Preface to the Japanese Version

Nancy Gaffield

My first encounter with Hiroshige Utagawa's "The 53 Stations of the Tokaido" was in a small arts shop in Eugene, Oregon in the 1970s. From that moment, the prints haunted me. Indeed, they were one of the reasons why I had to go to Japan, where I lived from 1979 to 84. The 'stories' in the poems are based on historical material, myth and legend, aspects of location, and personal memory, but they are also imagined accounts that cross the boundaries of time and place, building a bridge between worlds. As in the series of prints, there are 55 poems in the poetic series, with Nihonbashi representing the start and Kyoto the end. Ever since I first saw these prints, I have thought of them as poem-pictures. From Horace, the Latin phrase "ut picture poesis" (as is painting, so is poetry) describes a long tradition which dominated the theory of western art from the 17th to the end of the 18th century. Later, the Italian Petrarch contrived the idea of painting as mute poetry, poetry as the speaking picture. Thus, these poems are working within a long tradition whereby verbal art comments on the visual, and through them I hope to show how powerfully Hiroshige's art still resonates today.

When seeking a publisher for *Tokaido Road* in 2010, I dreamed of the poems appearing alongside Hiroshige's prints, but as this was my first collection, I knew no British publisher would take on such an expensive project. I also hoped that one day the poems might be published in Japan. Thanks to Kogakkan University, I have been able to realize that dream.

Tokaido Road has had a remarkably long life for a little book of poems. Published by CB editions in 2011, the book was nominated for the Forward First Collection Prize, and it won the Aldeburgh First Collection Prize. In 2012, Okeanos Ensemble commissioned me to write a libretto based on the poems for an opera, titled *Tokaido Road: A Journey after Hiroshige*, composed by Nicola LeFanu. The opera received its premiere at the Cheltenham Music Festival in 2014, and toured the UK in 2014 –15.

I want to thank Professor Hisayo Ikeda, who set up the Japan/UK Comparative Culture Workshop, and the people I met who studied and discussed my poems over two years. I have learned so much from them. In Ise, I enjoyed the greatest warmth and hospitality. I visited the Grand Shrine, and in the little shops of Okage Yokocho I kept seeing images and figures of frogs. I learned that the frog is a much-loved creature in poetry and art, and supposedly, has magical powers. The word "kaeru" means both "frog" and "return". Thanks to Kogakkan University, I have been able to return to this exceptional country and discover more deeply its long history and tradition. Most of all, I want to thank Professor Ikeda herself, whose energy, commitment, wisdom and skill in translation has made this book a reality.

日本語出版によせて

ナンシー・ガフィールド

　1970年代に、オレゴン州のユージーンの小さな美術店で、歌川広重の「東海道五拾三次」に初めて出会い、その瞬間からこの版画集の虜になってしまいました。その後この画集を求めて日本に渡り、1979年から84年まで日本に住むことになりました。この詩集に描かれた「様々な物語」は、史料、神話や伝説、土地の趣、そして個人的な思い出をベースにしたものですが、同時に、時間と空間の境を行き交って二つの世界に橋をかける想像上の話でもあります。広重の55枚の版画シリーズに合わせて、この詩集も日本橋から始まって京都で終わる55のシリーズ詩となっています。初めて目にしたときからずっと、これらの版画はわたしにとって「ポエム・ピクチャー（詩画）」だったのです。ホラティウス（64〜8 B.C）のラテン語の詩論のなかに「ウト　ピクトーレ　ポエーシス」（詩は絵のように）という成句がありますが、これは17世紀から18世紀にかけて西欧のアートシーンを支配した長い伝統を表すことばとなりました。のちに、イタリアのペトラルカ（1304〜74）から「絵は沈黙の詩のように、詩は語る絵のように」という発想が生まれました。ここに上梓した詩は、視覚芸術をことばの芸術で語るという西欧の長い伝統の中で培われたものです。この伝統を通して、今日においてもなお、広重の版画が力強く響き渡っていくことを、この詩集のなかで表現したいと思いました。

　2010年に脱稿した *Tokaido Road* を世に問うときには、なんとか広重の版画を入れて出版したいという夢をもっていました。しかし処女作の詩集であったために、英国では、そのような高価な本を出してくれる出版社が見つかりませんでした。そしてもう一つ、いつかこの詩集が日本で出版される日が来ることを願っていました。皇學館大学のおかげで、この夢を実現することができたのです。小さな詩集にしては、*Tokaido Road* は驚くほど息の長い作品となって現在に至っています。2011年にCBエディションから出版されると、優秀新作賞（フォワード・ファースト・コレクション賞）に推薦され、アルデブラ新作賞を受賞しました。2012年には、オケアノス室内合奏団（オケアノス・アンサンブル）から、詩集をもとにしたオペラ用のリブレット（台本）の執筆を委託され、ニコラ・レファノウ氏作曲による *Tokaido Road: A Journey after Hiroshige*（『東海道・ロード―広重の旅路をこえて』）という作品となりました。このオペラは2014年にチェルトナム音楽祭で初公演の栄誉を得て、2014年から15年にかけて、英国公演ツアーを行いました。

　日英比較文化研究会（JUCCW）を立ち上げられた池田久代教授、および、2年以上の時間をかけてこの詩集を学び鑑賞してくださった多くの方々に感謝いたします。研究会の方々からわたし自身も多くのことを学び、伊勢でいただいた最大級の温かいもてなしを心から楽しみました。神宮参拝の折、おかげ横丁の小さなお店にはカエルの絵や人形があちこちに並んでいました。カエルは（日本では）詩や絵画に登場する愛される生き物であることを知ったのもそのときでした。そして、おそらく、魔法の力をもつ生き物だということも。「かえる」には「カエル」と「帰る」という二つ意味があるといいます。皇學館大学のおかげで、わたしは世界に類をみないこの素晴らしい国に再び戻ってきて、この国の長い歴史と伝統をもっと深く発見することができたのです。中でもこの度、池田教授がこの作品に深く関わり、時間をかけ、知識と技術を駆使して邦訳の労を取られ、本書の出版を実現してくださったことに感謝いたします。

（翻訳：池田 久代）

凡例

一、 本書はナンシー・ガフィールド(Nancy Gaffield)の英詩集 Tokaido Road(2011)の全訳である。

一、 巻末の用語集は、若干の誤解が見られたり補足説明が必要な箇所には〔　〕で追加説明をした。

一、 本書に掲載した歌川広重の「東海道五拾三次之内」の版画は、かめやま美術館所蔵の保永堂版初刷を用いた。ただし、「桑名」は三重大学附属図書館より画像提供されたものである。

一、 作品名は本文中では、通称である「東海道五拾三次」と略記する。

一、 付録 CD の英詩の朗読は、詩人自身（ナンシー・ガフィールド）による。録音には、一部クリストファー・メイヨーの声も含まれる。

一、 付録 CD は、邦楽作曲家・中村洋一（都山流尺八大師範・竹山）作曲による『組曲・東海道五十三次』CD 四枚組全 55 曲（にはたづみレコード、2014）のうち Disc 1・4 より編集・収録した。

一、 表紙の題字は墨書家・吉田礼子による書き下ろし作品を用いた。

表　　紙：東海道五拾三次之内　庄野・白雨
デザイン：池田友里

目　　次
Contents

はじめに……………………………………………………………………………… i
Foreword

日本語出版によせて………………………………………………………………… ii
Preface to the Japanese Version

『東海道ロード』詩集（英語・日本語）……………………………………………1
Tokaido Road Collected Poems (English and Japanese)

用語集………………………………………………………………………………117
Glossary

解題
Commentary

    歌川広重の「東海道五拾三次」と *Tokaido Road* ── 青の往還 ──
                                                   岡野智子………122
    Hiroshige Utagawa's *Tōkaidō gojū santsugi* and *Tokaido Road* :
    A Dialogue in Blue   Tomoko Okano

    二つの東海道 ── 英詩『東海道ロード』と東西の邂逅 ──
                                                   池田久代 ……132
    Two Tōkaidōs : *Tokaido Road* and the Encounter between East and West
                                                               Hisayo Ikeda

訳者あとがきと謝辞………………………………………………………………142
Afterword and Acknowledgements by the Translator

執筆者紹介…………………………………………………………………………144
About the author, Nancy Gaffield, and the translator, Hisayo Ikeda

付録　『東海道ロード』詩の朗読
Appendix : DVD of Nancy Gaffield reading *Tokaido Road* with
Japanese musical accompaniment

東海道五拾三次之内
沼津・黄昏図
（部分）

Tokaido Road

Nancy Gaffield

CB editions

(オリジナル本)

本詩集は歌川広重の「東海道五拾三次」のシリーズ版画に対応して書かれた。(当該版画は下記の オンラインで鑑賞できる。) 東海道は日本の東西の首都を結ぶ街道で、版画は江戸 (東京) の日本橋 から始まり、京都の三条大橋で終着する。大名、将軍、巡礼、役者、芸人、旅人など、様々な人々が 東海道を旅した。版画の中の人物は単なる前景ではなく、それぞれの風景画の一部として描かれてい る。本詩集は絵画と詩歌を想像的に繋いで、旅の途中で出会う様々な登場人物、経験、記憶を捉えよ うとした。(ナンシー・ガフィールド)

　　　(www.hiroshige.org.uk/hiroshige/tokaido_hoeido.htm.)

詩集目次　Contents

1	Nihonbashi（日本橋）		29	Mitsuke（見附）
2	Shinagawa（品川）		30	Hamamatsu（浜松）
3	Kawasaki（川崎）		31	Maisaka（舞坂）
4	Kanagawa（神奈川）		32	Arai（荒井）
5	Hodogaya（保土ヶ谷）		33	Shirasuka（白須賀）
6	Totsuka（戸塚）		34	Futakawa（二川）
7	Fujisawa（藤沢）		35	Yoshida（吉田）
8	Hiratsuka（平塚）		36	Goyu（御油）
9	Ōiso（大磯）		37	Akasaka（赤阪）
10	Odawara（小田原）		38	Fujikawa（藤川）
11	Hakone（箱根）		39	Okazaki（岡崎）
12	Mishima（三島）		40	Chiryū（池鯉鮒）
13	Numazu（沼津）		41	Narumi（鳴海）
14	Hara（原）		42	Miya（宮）
15	Yoshiwara（吉原）		43	Kuwana（桑名）
16	Kanbara（蒲原）		44	Yokkaichi（四日市）
17	Yui（由井）		45	Ishiyakushi（石薬師）
18	Okitsu（興津）		46	Shōno（庄野）
19	Ejiri（江尻）		47	Kameyama（亀山）
20	Fuchū（府中）		48	Seki（関）
21	Mariko（丸子）		49	Sakanoshista（坂之下）
22	Okabe（岡部）		50	Tsuchiyama（土山）
23	Fujieda（藤枝）		51	Minakuchi（水口）
24	Shimada（島田）		52	Ishibe（石部）
25	Kanaya（金谷）		53	Kusatsu（草津）
26	Nissaka（日坂）		54	Ōtsu（大津）
27	Kakegawa（掛川）		55	Kyoto（京都）
28	Fukuroi（袋井）			

1   Nihonbashi

東海道五拾三次之内 日本橋・朝之景

All places exist in relation to Nihonbashi. Everything
begins here. Soft caps of the bay glimmer
in phosphorescent light. The men's breath disappears
into a grove of bamboo. Beneath their feet
stones awaken while overhead the vermilion bird
schooners south. Cursing and grumbling,
sandaled carriers regret the maiden chorus
of farewell, their silken scarves flushed with desire.

Inside, the edo-jin stir ashes to a dogged glow.
A pair of curs sniff the bridgehead and the rat
that passed there, now wallowing unreachable
in river silt. They turn their backsides
to our Hiro as he slips out of sight. The old town
droops into silence and the rains begin.

1　日本橋

　　　　すべての場所は日本橋につながる　すべてが

　　　　ここから始まる　入江の白波が　青白く

　　　　明滅し　男らの息は

　　　　竹林に消える　足もとで

　　　　石たちが目覚め　頭上では緋色の鳥が

　　　　帆船(スクーナー)のように南に向かう　ブツブツと乱暴な声で

　　　　草鞋(わらじ)ばきの棒手振りが　乙女らの別れの声を悼む

　　　　絹の襟巻きが欲望に染まる

　　　　家内では　江戸っこが灰をかいて火を熾(おこ)す

　　　　野良犬が二匹　橋のたもとでかぎまわり

　　　　通りかかったドブネズミが

　　　　手の届かない川の淀みでよたよたと転げまわる

　　　　愛しいヒロの姿が消えていくと　みんな踵(きびす)をかえして

　　　　古き街は沈黙にうなだれ　雨がふりだす

　　訳注
　　棒手振り＝天秤を担いでものを売り歩く商人たち

【日本橋について】
　江戸(東京)と京(京都)を結ぶ東海道には53の宿場が置かれ、人々は2週間かけて旅した。広重は、これらの宿場と江戸の日本橋と京都の三条大橋を含めた55の場所の風景、旅人やそこに住む人びとの楽しさ、侘しさを浮世絵木版画の連作に描いた。
　日本橋は街道の出発点であった。東海道だけでなく、江戸時代の五街道(東海道、中山道、日光街道、奥州街道、甲州街道)すべての起点であった。その日本橋を正面からとらえるという斬新な構想の図から広重の連作は始まる。橋の向こうからは、朝早く国元に帰る参勤交代の大名行列がやってくる。大木戸も開いたばかり。左には、魚河岸で仕入れた魚を掲げる魚屋や野菜売りの人々が朝の賑わいをみせる。様々な一日の始まりである。

2 Shinagawa

東海道五拾三次之内 品川・日之出

The bridge shivers with our passing.
Cheek by jowl houses ascend. Light seeps
through the gap between clouds and sea
reminding us that now the fishing's over.
I know I've been here before, know
without looking seven ships bob
on the surface, four trim their sails
before they slip out to sea, unobserved.
Someone reveals his hand: it's the ten of swords.
Nowhere to go but up.

Everything's happening on the roadside:
someone's boiling oden; vendors peddle souvenirs
of Shinagawa. Tea houses rub shoulders with
whore houses. A Tokyo drifter sits in a window
holding a fan, her face painted white with a pair
of heart-shaped lips. I want to tarry
but it is the fullness of time –
someone is waiting.

２　品川

渡ると橋がしなる
家々がひしめき　軒をならべた上り坂　雲と海の
隙間(すきま)に光が染み込んで
漁の終わりを告げる
いつかここに来たことがある　わたしには分るの ─
目には見えなくても ─ 水面に七艘の船が揺れ
四艘が帆をはって
海に滑り出していく　ひっそりと
誰かが手の内をさらすと ─ 剣の 10 の札だ
上に昇るより道がない

路上はなんでもござれ ─
おでんを煮るもの　品川土産を
売りあるくもの　茶屋と置屋(おきや)が
肩よせあう　江戸の流れ女がひとり
うちわをもって窓辺にすわっている
白塗りの顔に　赤い紅をさしたハートの唇
もっとここにいたいけれど　もう時がない ─
わたしを待つ人がいるから

訳注
劔の 10 ＝ タロットカードの「劔の 10」で、男の背中に 10 本の劔が刺さっているカード。後悔や自責の念を感じ、精神的に最悪の状況だが、少し光がさす。

【品川宿について】
　日本橋を出て最初の宿場が品川であった。歩いて 2 時間ほどの距離で、早朝発った大名行列も日の出頃の到着となる。図には、大名行列の後尾が描かれ、通りの右には出迎える役人たち、左には茶屋や旅籠が並ぶ。日本橋から一緒についてきた見送りも、品川の茶屋で別れの酒食をするのが常であったらしい。宿場には、飯盛り女（旅人のために給仕をする女中）という名目で旅籠に遊女を置くことを許されていた。図の左には、朝焼けの江戸湾（東京湾）。4 隻が帆を張って海に向かって動き出す。海岸線沿いの品川宿は風光明媚で知られていた。

3 Kawasaki

東海道五拾三次之内 川崎・六郷渡舟

Hunkering, Hiro abides by the rules,
waits to board at the recess of the river.
Tide hangs back with the ashes
of those who drowned at sea.

He shuffles out of sight. A ferryboat lures
the eye across the Tama, passengers wait
on the opposite bank before a cluster of houses
and a mule laden with barrels of sake.

Close to the distant shore a man on a raft searches
for a hole to cast his line. Hiro boards to cross
the border between this world and under. *If I plunge
into the river here will I quicken?*

Gulls and kingfishers sweep the surface clean of insects,
to the west clouds note the place the sun has pitched up.
All around the muddy marsh twisted pines grasp
for light, one by one rooftops clarify.

Change comes. First the earthquake,
then B29s. These hills
lopped for landfill. He tips the boatman
and wishes he'd stayed home.

3　川崎

　　　身をかがめて　ヒロは川の窪みで
　　　渡しの順番をまつ
　　　海の藻屑となった者たちの亡骸とともに
　　　潮が　たゆたう

　　　のろのろと　ヒロの姿が舟に消えると
　　　多摩川の向こうへと視線が誘われる
　　　向こう岸で　立て込んだ家々と酒樽の荷をのせたラバの前で
　　　舟客が待つ

　　　遥かな岸辺の浅瀬で　いかだに乗った男が
　　　釣り糸を垂らす深みを探す　ヒロは渡しに乗り
　　　この世と黄泉の境を渡る　もしここで川に飛び込んだら
　　　わたしは甦るだろうか

　　　かもめとカワセミが　水面をかすめて虫をさらえる
　　　西の方では　日の出の雲がたなびき
　　　沼地のあたり　松が身をよじって光りをもとめる
　　　少しづつ　屋根がはっきり見えてくる

　　　すべては移ろう　まずは地震
　　　それから　B29戦闘機　丘は
　　　埋め立て地へと消えていく　船頭に心付けをわたして
　　　ヒロはうなだれる　ああ　来なければよかった

【川崎宿について】
　東海道で最初の大河は多摩川で、多摩川を渡るあたりは六郷川と呼ばれ、そこを渡ると川崎宿に着いた。明治時代、重工業の発達のため東京湾の埋め立てが行われ、川崎も湾岸を利用した京浜工場地帯の中核となった。川崎市は、昭和17（1942）年4月18日の米軍による初めての本土空襲で攻撃目標になった。その後も何度も被害を受け、特に、昭和20（1945）年4月15日には200機余のB29による大規模な爆撃を受けた。

4 Kanagawa

東海道五拾三次之内 神奈川・台之景

Late evening clouds
are stained with indigo.
Minding the eaves
at the roofs' rim,
we heft up the hill.
A ribbon of blue
loops through the sky

TIME IS A CHANGER.

Through a carcass of trees the moon
looms. The seasons seize me too.
Old leaves thrown to earth
blame the tree, but new shoots
return from leavings.
Turn to the sun.

4　神奈川

　　　日暮れの雲が
　　　藍色に染まる
　　　張りだした庇に
　　　　　　ひさし
　　　気をつけながら
　　　足取り重く山路をいくと
　　　リボンのような青い輪が
　　　空に浮かぶ

　　　時はすべてを変えていく

　　　屍のような　木々の向こうに　月が
　　　しかばね
　　　ぼうっと現れる　わたしもまた季節に冒される
　　　木の葉は　恨みながら
　　　大地にもどるが　朽ち葉から
　　　新芽が蘇り
　　　太陽にむかう

【ヒロシゲ・ブルーについて】
　図の右手江戸湾を一望できる高台には茶屋や料理屋が軒を連ね、女たちが必死に旅人を引き込もうとする愉快な光景が見られる。左手には広い空と青い海。船の手前のきらきらと光る波うち際の模様が印象的である。広重の青、特に藍色の美しさは素晴らしく、海外では「ヒロシゲ・ブルー」とも呼ばれている。その青は、江戸時代後期にオランダ経由で輸入され、プルシアン・ブルー、あるいはベルリン・ブルー、また、それを略して「ベロ藍」とも呼ばれるものである。歌川広重や葛飾北斎など江戸後期の浮世絵師たちが好んで使用していた。
　画面の最上部に水平に引かれた真っ直ぐなぼかしは、「一文字ぼかし」または「天ぼかし」と呼ばれ、主に空を表現するための浮世絵の技法である。その色で季節や時間、天候などを表現し、藍は晴天、昼間。朱は秋、朝焼け、夕刻。墨は冬、雪、雨、夜を示す。

5 Hodogaya

東海道五拾三次之内 保土ヶ谷・新町橋

A stream at Hodogaya.
At the bridgehead a toothless fishwife
beckons the travellers
with sweetness. Operatic *irasshaimases*
from soba chefs in clouds
of broth, and then to cap it all
a chorus of slurps.

Satisfied customers.

Kikuyo opens her carriage and steps
out. Monks approach
from the execution grounds,
lure her in to amuse themselves.
A sign pointing to Kamakura reads:

Cultivate the joy of being rather than having.

5　保土ヶ谷

保土ヶ谷の　橋のたもとで
歯が抜けた粗野な女が
にこやかに　旅人を呼び込む
漂うだしの湯気ごしに　そば屋が
「(い) らっしゃい」と声を張り上げる
あげく　一斉に
蕎麦をすするコーラス

満足げな旅人たち

キクヨは籠をあけて外にでる
刑場からお出ましの
僧らが
いっしょにお楽しみをと　手招きする
「鎌倉へ」と道しるべ ―

なにはなくとも　今このときを楽しむべし

【保土ヶ谷宿について】
　図の手前にかかる帷子橋（新町橋）を渡ると保土ヶ谷宿である。橋の向こう側の「二八」とあるのは蕎麦屋の看板で、旅人たちを待ち構えている。
　死刑を行う場所である刑場は、平安時代から江戸時代にかけていくつか存在しており、保土ヶ谷宿から横浜港の方に下る保土ヶ谷道にも、暗闇坂刑場と呼ばれる神奈川奉公所の処刑場があった。その近くの願成寺には処刑された人の墓もある。

6 Totsuka

東海道五拾三次之内 戸塚・元町別道

These prints I first saw in Eugene in the spring of 1977. Observe the two-dimensional quality, the flatness of the picture-plane. What is seen is a mirror image. The text or image is drawn onto paper fixed to a piece of cherry wood, and then cut away according to the outline drawing. The carved woodblock is inked, and with the application of paper and pressure, a scene appears. The first of these are indigo but gradually monochrome evolves into brocade. I linger in the picture. Not the scenes of the demi-monde but the landscapes, where 'the individuality of nature is seen isolated from the entire', as Noguchi explained it in 1921. No longer valued after the war, they were borne overseas as wadding. Like them, I am always crossing the water.

> Totsuka's neon defeats the stars.
> I do not recognise the road
> in the print lined with shapely pines,
> today concrete stilts
> for the railway to DreamLand.
>
> She's there to receive me. *We waited*
> *for you*, she says, guides me in to the alcove,
> hands me a stick of incense
> to place before his photograph.
> We clap hands to summon his soul. She pours
> the spring sake, arranges fresh peonies,
> his cup overflows.
>
> *Remember – all existence is cyclical.*
> *See that we do not lose you.*

11

6　戸塚

　私がユージーンで初めてこの浮世絵版画に出会ったのは、1977年の春のことだった。二次元の本質である平坦な画の表面を覗き込むと、鏡像(ミラーイメージ)が見えて来る。桜材の版木に紙を乗せて文字や形を描き、輪郭線に沿って彫る。次に彫りを入れた版木に墨を塗り、その上に紙を当てて擦りつけると、場面が立ち現れる。藍色から刷りはじめ、徐々に単彩色から錦(にしき)へと変貌する。版画の中をさ迷うと、そこにあるのは花街の賑わいではなく、まぎれもなく風景(ランドスケープ)の世界だ。野口米次郎が1921年に解説したように、全体から切り取られた個としての自然がそこに在る。戦後になると浮世絵はすっかり廃れて、荷物の詰め物に使われて海を渡って行った。私も同じ。いつも海を渡っている。

　　　　戸塚のネオンが星を遮る
　　　　版画に描かれた美しい松並木は
　　　　どこに行ってしまったのだろう
　　　　今ではコンクリートの柱が立てられ
　　　　ドリームランドへと電車が走る

　　　　そこで女がわたしを迎える
　　　　お待ちしていました　と言いながら
　　　　わたしは　仏壇の前に導かれ
　　　　線香をわたされて　男の遺影に香を焚く
　　　　二人で手を合わせ　男の魂を呼びだす
　　　　女は牡丹の花を活け　春の酒を注ぐ
　　　　なみなみと

　　　　忘れないで ― いのちは巡るもの
　　　　あなたを失わせないで

訳注
ユージーン＝　米国オレゴン州西部の都市。
野口米次郎（1875-1947）＝明治から昭和にかけて英米で活躍した英詩人、小説家、評論家、俳句研究者。*From the eastern sea*（1903）をロンドンで刊行して好評を博し、1913年、オックスフォード大学の講師となり、松尾芭蕉の俳諧について論じ（『日本詩歌論』）、帰国後、『六代浮世絵師』などを刊行。
荷物の詰め物＝ 19世紀に版画が初めてヨーロッパに伝えられた時には、ここにあるように北斎漫画などのすり損じなどが荷物の詰め物や包装紙がわりに使われたが、20世紀の戦後には行われていない。
二人で手を合わせ＝ 原文は「手を打つ（clap hands）」であるが、この場面は神道ではなく、仏壇（仏教）なので、「手を合わせ」の意味と解した。

7 Fujisawa

東海道五拾三次之内 藤澤・遊行寺

After Ashbery's 'What Is Poetry'

As Hiroshige views it, a medieval temple with torii, mist settles
over the valley obscuring the houses, no place for blind men.

Tour groups with loudspeakers at the Order of the Wayfarer,
trying to recite *Namu Amida Butsu* for salvation.

The priest of the abandoned says to forsake family, desist
from lust. We are allowed only twelve personal items: rice bowl,

case for chopsticks, winter clothes, surplice, summer clothes
made of flax, handkerchief, sash, washi, string of beads, straw
    sandals,

cowl. Simply repeat the phrase: *Namu Amida Butsu*. The gate
marks transition from the sacred to the profane world, sign-
    posted

Enoshima Shrine where a milk-white nude with eight arms sits
    half-lotus,
female genitals exposed, playing a lute. And to the west a cave

called the womb where the holy one abides. The rare individual
nature reveals in isolation, Hiroshige in us all.

7　藤澤

アッシュベリーの「詩とは何か」を読んで

広重の目に映るは　鳥居のある中世の寺　谷に霧が降り
暗い家陰　盲人には向かない処

旅人がめざす本山では　ツアーグループが拡張器で
救いを求め　南無阿弥陀仏を唱えている

世を捨てた僧侶が諭(さと)す　家を捨て　煩悩を手放せ　と
生涯十二品目でこと足(た)れり ― 飯椀

箸箱　合わせ衣　短白衣(サープリス)
一重(ひとえ)の麻衣　手ぬぐい　帯　和紙　数珠　草鞋(わらじ)

そして頭巾　ひたすら　南無阿弥陀仏を　唱えよ
鳥居は聖俗の分かれ目 ― 立て札が立つ

江ノ島弁財天神社へと　八本の腕をもつ乳白色の裸体が半蓮華座で坐る
女性性器をあらわにして　リュウトを奏でる　西方に洞窟あり

聖なるものが住む母胎　稀有なる個の本質は
孤独のうちに出現する　だれの内にも住む　広重が

訳注
ジョン・アッシュベリー＝ John Ashbery (1927-2017) アメリカの前衛詩人、大学教授。20冊以上の詩集を出版し、ピューリッツァー賞、全米批評協会賞、全米図書賞など受賞多数。永年詩の実験に取り組んだアメリカ詩の泰斗。数年前にノーベル賞にノミネートされたが、2017年9月3日、90歳で死去。
八本の腕をもつ乳白色の裸体＝江ノ島弁財天には八臂弁財天（勝運守護）と妙音弁財天（音楽・芸能の守護）があるが、ここでは裸体でリュートを弾く妙音弁財天と八本の腕を持つ八臂弁財天のイメージが合体した表現になっている。この表現は著者による詩的イメージの創作であるので、原文の通りに訳した。

8 Hiratsuka

東海道五拾三次之内 平塚・縄手道

The road this morning doesn't say much,
it zigzags over water,
nuzzles the wind close to shore.
Picking algae at low tide, sea women scour
the mudflats, hanging it to dry in heavy sea air.
An old woman brushed by age
watches a courier run past
the breast of Mt Koma,
slice Fuji in half.

Now the real world rushes in with force.
I am an old woman seeking
a memory. I carried my daughter.
She rode my hip, heels spurring me
on, there were bruises. I clambered up
to the cave where the hermit lived,
handrailing branches and weeds.
We kept stopping among the wreck
and tangle of roots to listen for cricket-trill.
My breath came hard
as labour. I licked her salty seaweed hair,
caked with dried blood. Up here I was
on the rim of everything. I wanted to stay
until roots tendrilled my ankles, my back
became one with bark.

Instead, I joined the throng on the road
west, even as I heard a voice cry
   creeck   *creeck*

I was careful never to let my reflection play
on water, lest my soul leak out.
Too late. I am an old woman
found by a memory.

8　平塚

今朝の街道は　多くを語らず
水の上をジグザグと進み
風を岸辺に追いこむ
海草取りの女たちが
干潟をあさり歩いては　強いうみかぜに海草を干す
日に晒された老婆が
見つめている
飛脚が高麗山の山腹を走り去るのを
富士が半分に切れたところ

いま　現が　怒涛のように流れ込む
わたしは思い出をさがす老婆
娘を背負い　その踵にせかされて
青あざをつくり　小枝や草にしがみつきながら
隠者が住む山の洞窟に登った
残骸やもつれた木の根のあいだに佇んでは
コオロギの震える羽音に耳を澄まし
陣痛のように　息を荒げて
塩からい海草のような娘の髪を
血がこびりついたその髪を　舐めた
ここまで登りつめたけれど
もうこれまで　いつまでも
ここに居たかったのに
足首に木の根が巻きつき
樹皮と背中が ひとつになるまで

それも叶わず　旅人たちに混じって　西へと
旅を続けた　虫の音が聞こえてきても
　　　　　クリーク　　クリーク

わたしの影を水鏡に戯れさせないように
魂が漏れ出さないように
もう遅いのよ　わたしは老婆
あるのは思い出ばかり

9 Ōiso

東海道五拾三次之内 大磯・虎ヶ雨

Rain slashes black lines through a yellow sky at Ōiso. It is spring and I arrive at the haiku house to sit with Hiro at the foot of Tiger Stone. I think of him until a cat comes and circles himself into an O in the corner of the porch. Hiro's woman weeps in the opposite corner; big tears drop onto pages of her, rubbing out words. Her hands fumble her clothes seeking a handkerchief tucked inside the sleeve. It's three in the afternoon, too early to drink, too late to sleep. *I am lonelier than I have ever been*, she tells her companion on the other side. The cat says nothing, no one on the road. Hills, sea, trees – all blackness.

>   May 28 and rain heavy as ever on this day
>   Tora-gozen lost her lover.*
>
>   Bright coast with sunlight
>   travellers flood the road
>
>   Rains surge
>   poems return

* The rain falling in this print is significant. Tora-gozen was the 12th-century mistress of Soga-no-juro. The pair killed a government official at Ōiso in order to avenge the death of her father. Her lover, Juro, was killed and Tora herself turned into a stone. Each year the stone is said to weep on the anniversary of Juro's death, and it is believed that the rain on this day is Tora's tears. There is also a famous house where poets come to write haiku here.

9　大磯

　大磯の黄色い空から雨が黒い槍のように打ちつける。今は春。俳句館までやってきて、わたしはヒロと虎石のそばに座る。ヒロのことを考えていると、猫が一匹やってきて、ポーチの隅でクルクル回って丸くなる。ヒロの女が向こう側の隅ですすり泣く。大粒の涙が本の頁に落ちて、文字が消えていく。女は袖に押し込んだハンケチを探そうと両手で着物を弄る。午後の三時。酒を飲むには早すぎるし、そんなに遅くまで寝てもいられない。こんなに寂しかったことはないわ、と女はこちらの道連れに語りかける。猫は泣かず、道の人影も消えた。丘と海と木々 ― みんな闇のなか。

　　　　陰暦の五月二十八日には、いつも、激しい雨が降る
　　　　虎御前が愛しい人を失った日＊

　　　　陽光の眩しい岸辺の道には
　　　　旅人たちが溢れ

　　　　雨はうねり
　　　　詩がもどる

原注
＊この版画の降りしきる雨には意味があります。虎御前は鎌倉時代（12世紀）の蘇我十郎の愛妾でした。二人は大磯で、虎の父の仇討ちのために幕府の役人を殺害しました。愛する十郎は斬り死し、虎は死んで石に身をやつしました。毎年、十郎の命日には、その石が呻き泣くのです。この日の雨は「虎ケ雨（涙）」と言い伝えられるようになりました。この地にはまた、俳人たちが集う有名な俳句の館があります。

10 Odawara

東海道五拾三次之内 小田原・酒匂川

Wide river and no bridge,
the carriers sprout wings,
enter the river avoiding whirlpools
and the threat of drowning.

Choked by a cloud of midges
the men are oiled and plumed.
Carp swoosh between
the spokes of their legs.

The passenger watches
from her cushioned perch, cradles
crickets in a bamboo cage. Inside
her own, a bleating cry.

The river pumps and gathers
speed, toes fathom the contours,
water colours, saffron-veined
mother lode.

Her heart now the weight of a feather,
paradise, but first this long
journey with many gates
to the field of offerings.

10　小田原

広い川には橋がない
人足が翼のように腕を突きだして
渦に足を取られないように　溺れないように
川に入る

小魚が群がるので
人足たちは　泊をひいて羽づくろいをする
鯉が脚の間をすり抜ける　シュ　シュ
車輪の輻(スポーク)をすり抜けるように

乗り客は見つめる
座布をしいた止まり木の上で
竹籠に入れたコオロギを　そっと揺する
心のなかで　シクシクと泣く声

川は水嵩を増し　早瀬となる
つま先が　川底の輪郭を測り
水の色　サフラン色の血管
母なる鉱脈をなぞる

女の心は羽毛のように軽い
極楽浄土　だがその前に　長い旅路がつづく
供物の野へと続くあまたの門を
くぐり抜けて行かなければならない

【小田原宿について】
　小田原は、江戸を出て初めての城下町であり、難所と言われている箱根山の前の宿場であった。小田原宿に入るには手前に位置する酒匂川(さかわ)を渡らなければならなかった。水量が減ずる10月から2月までは仮橋を架け、水量が増す3月から9月までは徒行渡し(かちわた)(歩いて渡る)となる。その渡し方は、駕籠に乗った武士を大勢がかつぐ大高欄輦台、梯子に板をのせた平輦台、さらに肩車など身分に応じていろいろであった。

11 Hakone

東海道五拾三次之内 箱根・湖水図

Did the face of the ridge change as we climbed
higher, avoiding the knife edge?
These peaks are unforgiving.

Your outstretched hand sparks
a crackling between us.
I will not let you go.

From the bough of the black pine
the cry of a shrike pierces the sky.
Night advances on the lake below.

Too late to ask
did we have to travel this far.
Path succumbs to thicket, to sedge.

Grey haze shields the valley.
I believe you are just ahead,
I will find you.

11 箱根

　　　　ナイフのような山の端を避けながら　高くたかく登ると
　　　　尾根の様相は変わったか
　　　　峯々に容赦はない

　　　　あなたの差し出す手と　この手が
　　　　火花をちらす
　　　　あなたを行かせはしない

　　　　黒松の枝から
　　　　百舌(もず)の声が　空を突き刺す
　　　　下の湖に　夜の帳(とばり)がおりる

　　　　今さら問うても甲斐(かい)ないが
　　　　こんなに遠くまで　一緒に旅をしなければならなかったのか
　　　　道が　雑木林からスゲの茂みへと消えていく

　　　　灰色の靄が谷をおおう
　　　　あなたはすぐ先にいるはず
　　　　きっと追いつくから

訳注
百舌の声＝モズは小動物を捕食にとる。秋になると獲物を木の枝に刺して速贄(はやにえ)をつくる習性があり、長い尾を振りながら、キイキイキチキチと鋭い声で高鳴きをする。

【箱根・湖水図】
　様々な色でモザイクのように描かれた岩山が芦ノ湖の方にそそり立つ。その岩間の道を大名行列が進む様子が描かれている図からは、箱根越えの険しさが伝わる。湖の向こうには白い富士が描かれ、色彩と構図が印象的である。

12 Mishima

東海道五拾三次之内 三島・朝霧

Trees travel in groups, forgetting
their shadows. In morning mist

they resemble strips of black paper.
Horse and rider, like the old

beliefs, have never gone away. Yesterday
we crossed Hakone Pass. Hard going,

no get-out. It's our own fault – we sat up
playing Go under a sky brimming with

reflected Sirius, woke to a world of silence
and mist. Everything arbitrary,

like the mature geisha in a bad economy –
if only Townsend Harris had stayed home.

But oh no he just had to come, see and pry
the monster open, swallow it whole – pearl and all.

Horse and rider emerge from the mist.
Hiro's heard the women of Mishima are beautiful

but take too much time with their make-up.
53 steps to Dharma.

12　三島

木々は群れをなして旅をする　みずからの
陰を忘れて　朝霧のなかで

陰は黒い短冊のように見える
人馬は　昔ながらの

信念のように　消えたことがない　昨日
箱根の剣を越えた　辛い山越え

逃げ場もなく　あれは過ちだ —
二人で寝ずに　碁を打った　シリウスの光溢れる空の下で

沈黙と山霧の世界で目覚めた
すべては気の向くまま

年増の貧乏芸者のように —
タウンゼント・ハリスなど来なければよかったのに

何たること　わざわざ覗き見に来ただけとは
怪物があんぐりと口を開けて　丸呑みにするのを — 真珠もろとも

人馬が霧の中から姿を現す
三島の女は美しい　とヒロは聞いたことがある

が　化粧に時間をかけすぎる
ダルマ(さとり)まで五十三歩

訳注

タウンゼント・ハリス（1804-1878）＝米国の外交官。日本の江戸時代後期に訪日し、日米修好通商条約を締結したことで知られる。初代駐日総領事 (1855-58)、初代駐日大使（1858-61）

ダルマ（悟り）まで53歩＝『華厳宗入法界品』における仏教説話で、善財童子（インドの長者の息子）は発心して、55箇所を訪ね歩き、道中53人の善知識に出会った。善財童子は最後に普賢菩薩に出会って浄土往生を願い菩薩となった。江戸時代に徳川家康が江戸と京都の間に53の宿場（東海道）を置いたのは、東の江戸（穢土）から西の京都（浄土）への信仰（求道）の道を目指しての善知識の数とも考えられている。

【三島宿と三島大社】
　三島は、箱根山を超えてきた旅人やこれから越えようとする旅人たちで、夜明け前から夜遅くまで賑わっていた宿場であった。図は、早朝三島大社の前を旅人たちが出発する様子を描いている。彼ら以外の背景や左側の旅人たちは、墨と青の2色のシルエットで表わされ、宿場を霧がつつみこむ静かな様子が伝わってくる。
　三島大社からは、伊豆半島を南へ天城峠を越え下田に至る下田街道が始まる。タウンゼント・ハリスは、下田に入港したのち通商交渉のため江戸に向かう際には、この街道を通り三島を経由した。

三嶋大社　（平成 30 年 3 月撮影）

13 Numazu

東海道五拾三次之内　沼津・黄昏図

The kanji says a pilgrim bound for Kompira
walks beside Kano River. On the farthest shore

a curtain of trees guards Yamabushi tengu, forest
goblin who speaks without moving his lips.

Regret and departure. Sleeves soaked in tears.

I walk forward turning round, like the pilgrim
who carries a mask on his back. A votive gift

for the guardian of seafarers. Harvest moon rises,
kindles the gauze of my dress. Ashes swirl

through trees. I sweep the garden clean of leavings,
count fireflies as they glide from trunk to trunk, contemplate

the surety of things, one thousand eight hundred sixty-eight
   steps
to the small shrine at the top where Hiro is now.

13　沼津

　　金比羅詣での巡礼は　狩野川ぞいの道をいく
　　と漢字の道しるべ　遥か彼方の川岸の

　　鬱蒼とした木立が　山伏天狗を守っている
　　口を動かさずにものを言う　森の妖怪

　　別れを惜しみ　袖が涙にぬれる

　　わたしは　振り返りながら　前へと進む
　　背中にお面を背負って歩く　巡礼のように

　　船乗りの守り神に奉納する供え物
　　中秋の月が昇り　薄絹の衣を明るく照らす

　　木立の間を灰が舞う　わたしは庭をはき清めながら
　　幹のあいだを飛び交う蛍を数え　じっと見つめる

　　確かなものを　ヒロのいる頂上の小さな社まで
　　あと千八百六十八段

訳注
山伏天狗＝天狗は日本人の霊魂観から生まれた霊的存在で、善悪の二面性（山神山霊と怨霊）を持つ。山伏（修験道）は山間部で苦行・精進の修行をするうちに、山神と一体化して超人的験力をもつに至った。こうして民間伝承の中で、天狗と山伏が同一視され、山伏の出で立ちをした山伏天狗の概念ができた。

【金毘羅参り】
　大きな満月が上がり、狩野川沿いの道を旅人と親子が、沼津の宿場に向かって歩いている。白い行衣に天狗面を背負うのが、金比羅参りの独特の習俗であったらしい。巡礼の親子が手に柄杓を持っているのは、施しを受けるための物である。江戸時代、庶民が旅することは禁じられていたが、金毘羅参りと伊勢のお陰参りだけは許されていた。

14 Hara

東海道五拾三次之内　原・朝之富士

Eighty miles from Edo, Fuji's peak escapes
the picture frame, squats shadowless
above a plateau of over-ripe grass.

Nothing but white light and the thin scream
of cranes ascends through a window to
a liquid world, a delicate day,
two women travelling alone.

Half-asleep clouds in an overcast sky,
and long tufts of September grass brush the blue
silk of her dress. They are going nowhere,
cranes too just hanging around.

A sudden chill on the nape says time
to walk on. Somewhere a lone wolf
lopes through the reeds. *Wolves are patient*
remarks one crane to the other.

The breeze shakes loose the folds of her
kimono, a pale blue thigh, bedewed. *Let's wait
for the wind to drop, lie down
in the long grass and amuse ourselves.*

We are miles from anywhere.

14　原

江戸から三十三里　富士の高嶺が画縁から
突き出し　草の生い茂る高原に聳(そび)えて
影もなく　うずくまる

白い光と　鶴の微(かす)かな鳴き声だけが
画縁をぬけて登っていく
流体の世界へと　心地よい一日
ふたり連れの女旅

かき曇った空に　まどろむ雲
九月の長草の茂みが　女の青い絹のキモノを
なでる　二人はどこへいくともなく
鶴もただ　ぐずぐずとたむろする

突然　頸筋(くびすじ)に冷気が走り　先を急げと　うながす
どこかで　一匹狼が
芦間(あしま)を駆ける　― 狼たちは辛抱づよいわね ―
一羽の鶴がもう一羽に話しかける

風が　そよと女の裾を揺らし
白い腿をあらわにする　露にぬれた腿を　待ちましょう
風が凪ぐのを　長い草に身を横たえて
楽しみましょう

ここは人里離れたところ

【日本画の手法と絵師の遊び心】
　浮島ケ原から仰ぐ富士山の山頂が図の枠から突き出ていることで、その雄大さが表現されている。27 掛川の図では、凧が図の枠からはみ出て描かれているが、画面を完結したものとせず枠を超えて中と外とがつながる構図は、日本画特有の視点のひろがりや動きを感じさせる手法。両掛けを担ぐ男の着物には、広重の片仮名の「ヒロ」を菱形に組み合わせた模様が描かれている。この柄は他の図にも見られるので、気を付けて見てみるのも面白い。

15 Yoshiwara

東海道五拾三次之内　吉原・左富士

Three riders atop one horse leave Hara in a blizzard
of seed and insect. At mid-morning they pass daimyō
wives held hostage by the shōgun tearing pine bark
with their fingernails. A web straddles the path,
orb-weaver hangs at the hub. Buddha in the undergrowth
measures the distance to Yoshiwara.

Hato bus, old dream-maker, halts before the bridgehead;
travellers order oolong tea, show photos
of Fuji framed by snow-clad pines, Fuji topped with new
moon rising. I find the bus stop named Hidari Fuji
in the kink of the road, no Mt Fuji, just a factory
and a mansion where Fuji should be.

Travellers on the Tokaido
meander between
centuries. Fuji doesn't change.

15　吉原

　馬にのった三人の旅人は　種や昆虫が群れ飛ぶなか
原を後にして　午前半ば　大名の奥方たちを追い抜いていく
将軍の人質になる女たちが　爪で松の樹皮を掻きむしる
クモの巣が道をまたぎ
まん中にオニグモがぶら下がる　薮のなかで仏陀が
吉原への道のりを測る

夢のはとバスは　橋のたもとで止まる
旅人は烏龍茶を注文し　富士の写真を見せあう
雪化粧の松に縁どられた　富士のうえに新月が昇る
道を曲がったあたりに「左富士」という名のバス停があるのだが
富士があるはずの場所に　富士は見えない
あるのはただ工場とマンションばかり

東海道の旅人は
世紀をこえて　うねり歩くが
富士は変わらない

訳注
はとバス＝東京都内、神奈川県の定期観光バスの名前

【吉原宿について】
　東海道を江戸から京に向かうとき、富士山は右手に見えるが、この辺りでは道が曲がりくねり左に見えてくる。松の並木を透して見る富士は絶妙であったらしい。現在では、周辺には製紙工場や住宅が立ち並び、一本の松だけが残されている。

16 Kanbara

東海道五拾三次之内　蒲原・夜之雪

I cross the border of snow at night,
breathe in the picture.

Winter stars coalesce with snowflakes,
station hushed by snow,

a figure under a half-opened umbrella
follows footsteps down the slope.

A shutter opens on an old man crazy
with painting. Summer evening

succulent with crickets and the peonies'
perfume. She sits in the doorway, her kimono

akimbo, indigo butterflies on white linen long
to flee to the safety of flowers; she tries

not to move, her eyes reveal nothing,
but in failing light he intercepts

the wildness in her. A sudden gust of wind
disturbs the distance between us.

The shutter closes on three figures
in the foreground dressed in snow.

16　蒲原

夜　わたしは雪の境を超えて
版画の中で息をする

冬の星が雪片に溶け
宿場は雪に沈む

半開きの傘をさした人影が
足あとをたどって坂を下る

雨戸が開き　画狂の老人が見える
夏の黄昏(たそがれ)どき

咽(むせ)ぶようなコオロギの声と牡丹の香り
女が戸口に座っている　キモノを

はだけて　白い麻衣のうえの藍色の蝶々は
安全な花のもとに帰りたいと焦(こ)がれる　女は

身動きもせず　虚ろな目をしている
だが　微かな光の中で　男が押しとどめる

女の狂気を　突然　一陣の風が吹いて
わたしたちの距離を　かき乱す

雨戸が閉じて　雪化粧の前景に
三人の人影が見える

【蒲原の雪】
　深々と雪がつもる静かな寂しい夜を描いたこの図は、広重の代表作として知られる。蒲原は豪雪地帯でなく、むしろ温暖な地であるので、この図は広重による虚構ではないかと言われている。

17 Yui

東海道五拾三次之内　由比・薩埵嶺

At Yui, travellers had a choice: risk drowning at sea or death by bandits
　　on Satta Pass. In the garden this morning kill-fish lap
　　their bowl indifferent to crows balancing on the rim.
　　Ack-ack-ack-ack, crows laugh as they watch fish loop-the-loop.

Kikuyo shivers thinking of travellers peaky as an August moon,
　　too close to the edge, torn between safety and danger.
　　Trees fall away from the blue-green waters of Suruga,
　　four junks head for the point of vanishing.

A grey thought clings to the ledge. He has forgotten. *I am not jealous,
　　though I know he's not alone*, Kikuyo thinks. She paints
　　her bottom lip and chooses the high road. Leaves
　　at once as clouds unravel the day.

17　由比

由比では　旅人は選択を迫られる ― 海で溺れ死ぬか
　　　　それとも　薩埵峠(さったとうげ)の山賊に襲われるか
　　　― 今朝　庭の金魚鉢のメダカが跳ねた　梢のカラスを気にもとめず
　　　魚の宙返りをみて　カラスが笑う　カーカー　カー

キクヨは身震いする　八月の月のようなやつれた旅人を想って
　　　ああ　後がない ― 生と死の間で引き裂かれ
　　　木々が駿河湾の青い海からそり返り
　　　四艘の帆船が水平線に消えていく

岩棚に憂鬱(ゆううつ)がこびりつく　忘れられてしまった　あの男に　嫉妬なんか
　　　　しないわ　あんたは誰かと一緒だろうけど　キクヨは思案する
　　　下唇に紅をさし　峠の路(ハイロード)を選ぶ
　　　雲行きを見て　すぐに発ちましょう

【薩埵(さった)峠について】
　由比宿と興津宿の間に位置する薩埵峠は難所で知られていた。その頂上あたりにさしかかると、突然雄大な富士が見える。図に描かれている峠を行く三人、そのうち旅人の二人は断崖絶壁の崖の上でその富士山を眺めている。
　この峠は江戸初期（1655・1658）に開かれたが、それ以前はこの峠を越すには波打ち際を通る危険な道を行かなければならなかった。波の合間を縫って一気に通り抜けるときには、親子でも思いやる余裕がないことから、この道は「親知らず子知らず」と呼ばれた。現代では、峠の眼下には、駿河湾にせり出すようにカーブを描く東名高速が、東海道本線と国道１号と交差し、その景色も見ごたえがある。

18   Okitsu

東海道五拾三次之内　奥津・興津川

Fit for service four men ford the river at Okitsu,
bearing sumō and sputtering

yoisho

yoisho

yoisho

Water soothes aching legs. The one they carry,
Man Mountain, sits with folded arms, satisfied
smile, the other on his horse gazes out to sea.

Tonight they will enjoy a good soak with maiko,
trained to rub shoulders and loins,
accomplished in the art of shampooing.

18　奥津

　　　興津では　四人の人足が川を渡る
　　　力士を担いでバシャバシャと

　　　　　　　　　　　　　　　　　　ヨイショ
　　　　　　　　　　ヨイショ

　　　　　　　　　　　ヨイショ

　　　水をいくのは有り難い　ひとりは山のような大男
　　　腕組みしてご満悦　ニコニコと駕篭に乗る
　　　もうひとりは　馬の背で　海を眺めている

　　　今夜は　宿でお楽しみ
　　　まいこのサービス付き
　　　腰肩揉みでも湯浴みでも　どれもこれもお手のもの

訳注
まいこ＝ここでは、飯盛り女（2.品川参照）

【奥津・興津川】
　図は、二人の相撲の力士を乗せた興津川の徒歩渡の光景である。彼らは刀を腰にさしているところから、武士の身分で取り立てられた大名のお抱え力士と考えられる。江戸時代は、寺社の建築や修繕などの募金を目的とした勧進相撲があり、そのための移動中かもしれない。

19 Ejiri

東海道五拾三次之内　江尻・三保遠望

Miho peninsula pushes into Suruga Bay,
white sand treads the heels of ancient pines.

The feather mantle flutters and quivers
about her shoulders

yellow lustrous as the full moon at perigee
illumines wave-lap, shadows pines

orbed by a waning moon,
a pair of herons rise east towards Hara

now a crescent as waves recede,
geese fly backwards and fall into the sea

new moon and darkness, clouds part
to show a globe of light.

I am ablaze for you

•

On a sea flecked with lanterns
Nakuryo joins his friends to fish by firelight.

A yellow feather falls from his sleeve.*

* In the Noh play 'The Feather Mantle' (Hagoromo) a fisherman finds a magic feather mantle belonging to a spirit ('tennyo'). The tennyo demands its return, for without it she cannot fly back to heaven. He finally agrees, if she will dance for him. The dance is symbolic of the phases of the moon, and in the finale she disappears like a mountain that is slowly covered in mist. Today's visitors to Miho no Matsubara can see the 650-year old pine where the five-coloured kimono was discovered.

19　江尻

　　　三保半島が駿河湾に突き出し
　　　白砂が古松の根を踏む

　　　羽衣がはためき揺れる
　　　女の肩のあたりに

　　　満月のような　つややかな黄色い羽衣が
　　　ひたひたと寄せる波を照らし　松に陰を落とす

　　　欠けゆく月の弓のなかを
　　　二羽の鷺が飛び立ち　原へと向かう

　　　浪が引くと　三日月
　　　雁が後ずさりして　海に落ちていく

　　　新月と闇　雲は分かれて
　　　光の輪がみえる

　　　　　　あなたのために燃えているのよ
　　　・
　　　炎がまだらに光る海で
　　　ナクリョウは仲間らと　漁火(いさりび)の漁をする

　　　ひとひらの黄色い羽が　男の袖から落ちる *

原注
* 能楽の「羽衣」では、漁師が天女の持ち物である羽衣を見つける。天女は羽衣がないと天に戻れないので、返して欲しいと懇願する。漁師はついにその頼みを聞き入れ、その代わりに自分のために舞を舞うように所望する。月の諸相を象徴する舞が終わると、ゆっくりと霧に包まれていく山のように、天女は姿を消す。三保の松原を訪れる旅人たちは、今でも650年前の老い松を見ることができる。その枝に五色に彩られた羽衣が掛かけられていたという。

訳注
ナクリョウ＝美保の松原に住む漁師の白龍（ハクリョウ）のこと。この詩では「ナクリョウ」と読ませている。
・（文中の黒丸）＝書道の余白に散った墨の点（したたり）のような効果を持つ。時や場面の移行を示唆する。

三保の松原にある羽衣の松
（平成 27 年 5 月撮影）

初代の「羽衣の松」は1707年の宝永噴火の際に海中に沈んだとされている。二代目の羽衣の松も樹齢650年を越えて衰弱が激しく、2010年に現在の三代目の松に世代交代をした。

美保の松原から仰ぐ富士山

20 Fuchū

東海道五拾三次之内　府中・安倍川

Who's this moving towards me?
Men and horses entering the river's belly.

Away from the bank we see
sweetfish feast on waterweed,
clear water.
The current butters us up,
lures us in.
Mind my weft and I will let you pass.

The river churns,
we shamble through silt where eels spawn,
reeds ribbon our ankles,
we don't fall.

Out here feels different,
mauve changes to green,
it's hard to swim,
fish swish –
we twist to grab hold,
she slips away.

Trust me to steer you clear of the shuttles.

Slick as newborns
we scuttle up the bank,
crawling mewling shaking off
spume, glad for land,
sad for what we've left behind.

20　府中

　　　　　　　　わたしの方に近づいてくるのは誰？

馬と人足が川のふくらみに入っていく

岸から離れたところでは
アユが川藻のごちそうにありつく
澄んだ水
流れがわたしたちをおだててては
水のなかに誘う
　　　　　　わたしの流れ(ウエフト)に気をつけて　そうすれば通してあげるわ

川が泡立つ
うなぎが産卵する泥のなかを　ヨロヨロと進む
足首に葦が絡みつくが
躓いたりしない

ここまで来ると　あたり一変
ふじ色が緑にかわり
泳ぐに泳げない
魚がかすめとおる ──
掴もうと身をよじると
するりと身をかわす
　　　　　　大丈夫　引き波(シャトル)に当たらないように連れて行ってあげるわ

赤子のように濡れて　滑りながら
わたしたちは岸によじ登る
這うように　泣きながら　泡をふり払い
岸に辿りつく　嬉しくもあり
残してきたものが　悲しくもあり

訳注
流れ、引き波(ウエフト)(シャトル) = 'weft' と 'shuttles' の原義はそれぞれ「織物の横糸」「織機の杼(ひ)」であるが、水面下の言及のため、訳語としては海事用語を用いた。

21 Mariko

東海道五拾三次之内　丸子・名物茶屋

A rush hut shelters beneath
a rose-coloured sky,
weather-worn stones lead up
to yam broth amidst young leaves.
Not one to brood, Mariko straps
the baby to her back, makes ready
for the travellers coming soon.

*Here is the dewy path
to leave our cares behind*,
Hiro says as he hands her a single
camellia. She bites the head
off, places the stem in a vase,
petals beneath. One time,

one meeting. A wooden well,
bamboo lid, tabi slide
across tatami, water
simmers, tap
of tea spoon, whisking.
Hiro tastes the tea with his ears,
Mariko enjoys the privilege
of service. *The tea is very nice*,
he wipes the lip of his cup once
with two fingers,
places it upside down.

Plum tree bursts into blossom.
Ah, this floating fleeting world!

21　丸子

茜空(あかねぞら)のした　藁葺き屋根の茶屋
古びた路傍の石畳に導かれ
新緑のあたりに漂う
おいしい汁の匂いに誘われる
なにくわぬ顔で ―
マリコは赤ん坊をおんぶして
旅人たちの到着を待つ

*露地*では
煩いごとはしばし忘れよう
椿を一輪　渡しながら
ヒロが言う　女は花を嚙み切って
茎を壺に挿す
床に花びらが散る　一期

一会　木枠の井戸
竹の蓋　足袋が滑るように
畳を横切る　釜の水が
チラチラと沸き　茶杓を
打ち　茶筅をまわす
ヒロは耳で茶を味わう
マリコは茶を立てる喜びに
ひたる　*結構なお点前茶ございます*
男は二本の指で
茶碗のふちをいちどぬぐい
茶碗を返して裏を拝見

にわかに　梅の花がひらく
あー　移ろいゆく　儚き　浮き世よ！

訳注
おいしい汁の匂い＝丸子名物のとろろ汁のこと
露地＝茶庭（茶の湯の草庵式茶室につけた庭）

22 Okabe

東海道五拾三次之内　岡部・宇津之山

Kikuyo enters the defile at nyubai,
the start of the rainy season

      Is the one I love alive
      out there?

Crow answers

      Skraww

Road contracts in the cleavage of Okabe pass,
ivy scrolls up trunks, throttles light

Tengu turns up in the bones
of the hillside,
wind combs the pines
sets needles spinning

      I know where you are
      there floating in air

Deep in the forest
high up the mountain
iris bloom
the road thickens
with maple branch and vine
traveller with the mask
on his back

      Is the one I love
      up here somewhere?

Wood thrush replies *kiskadee*
kata kata kee

22　岡部

キクヨは入梅のころ　隘路(あいろ)にむかう
雨の季節が始まる

　　　　恋しい人は　向こうで
　　　　無事かしら？

烏が応える
　　　　カー　　カー

岡部の峠の谷間　狭い径に
ツタが幹にからみつき　光をさえぎる

天狗が　現れる
山腹の骨のなかに
風が松を櫛けづり
松葉がクルクルと舞う

　　　　分かっているわ　あんたがどこにいるのか
　　　　ほら　そこ　宙に浮かんでいるわ

森の奥深く
山の高みに
菖蒲(あやめ)の花が咲く
道端には
楓の枝や蔦が生い茂り
お面を背負った
旅人が行く

　　　　恋しい人は
　　　　ここいら辺まで来たかしら？

森の鶫(つぐみ)が応える　キスカデー
カタ　カタ　キー

23 Fujieda

東海道五拾三次之内　藤枝・人馬継立

Then it rained. Not a soft spring rain
but a hammering, bad weather.

May rains, swift current,
no crossing Oikawa

Tokaido black spot.

Rain throbs on, river
breathes – *no one even knows
I have a story to tell.*

> *My fish have lovely fins,
> they rarely flounder.*

Rice-paper skin glows
iridescent copper and gold.

> *My fish are coy.*

Their long whiskers tremble
as they brush the naked flesh
of men carrying men.

> *I am patient,
> my fingers spread
> across the plain
> reading you.*

23　藤枝

　　それから雨がきた　やわらかい春の雨ではなく
　　木槌で打つような　悪天候

　　五月の雨　激流
　　大井川が渡れない

　　東海道の難所

　　雨が叩きつけ　川が
　　息をする — 誰にも分からないのよ
　　わたしにだって語りたいことがある

　　　　　わたしの魚には　美しいヒレがあるの
　　　　　だから　ヒラメのように　もがいたりしない

　　和紙のような皮膚が輝く
　　赤銅色(あかがね)　金色(こんじき)の虹のように

　　　　　わたしの魚は恥じらうこひ

　　客を担ぐ人足の裸のからだを
　　掠めると
　　こひの長いひげが震える

　　　　　わたしは　辛抱強く
　　　　　手を広げて
　　　　　広野を渡る
　　　　　あなたの気配を探し求めて

訳注
和紙＝原文のライスペーパーは、通草紙（カミヤツデを原料にした薄い上質紙）であるが、米国では一般的に和紙をさす。

24 Shimada

東海道五拾三次之内　島田　大井川駿岸

At last the day dries out,
travellers delirious
to be on the river again.

The river scrambles and splits,
breechclothed coolies flex muscles,
manganese herons follow
runnels, fracture the surface
and come up clean.

I want you to connect the image
with the human story.

Wide and treacherous, water waist-deep
and rising –
daimyō in palanquin, samurai
on a litter, peasants piggy-backed.

> *Lose your footing now*
> *and you are mine, I*
> *will take you away to Suruga Bay.*

Anyone could see the shōgun was beaten.
Anyone could see bridges would be built.

24　島田

やがてすっかり　一日が干からびて
旅人たちは　半狂乱
もういちど　川を渡りたいと

川がどっと押し寄せ　裂けるたび
褌姿の人足らは　手足の筋肉を緊張させ
灰白色の鷺は
細流で　川面に突っ込んでは
さっと首をもち上げる

あんたに伝えて欲しいのよ
この一部始終を

荒れ狂うこの川のことを　腰まで水に浸かる
水嵩は　なおも増えていく──
大高欄にのった大名　輦台のサムライ
百姓たちは背におわれ

　　さあ　足を滑らせたら
　　あんたはわたしのもの
　　駿河湾に連れ去ってあげる

将軍だって　屈する時がくる
橋だって　架けられる時がくる

訳注
大高欄＝江戸時代に大名・貴人を駕籠のまま載せて川を渡る台。20〜30人で担いだ。
輦台＝川を渡る客を乗せた台。普通、板に2本の担い棒をつけたもので、4人で担いだ。
屈する時がくる＝徳川幕府の政策（入り鉄砲に出女など）で東海道の川に橋をかけない場所があることを示唆した表現。

25 Kanaya

東海道五拾三次之内　金谷　大井川遠岸

You are never far from my thoughts.
I remember you on your raft of oleander
and chrysanthemum, women weeping
on the banks, I soaked the hems of their silks,
carried you from Totomi Bank
to my depths
we lay down together
you were mine at last.

I am a remnant
river, I remember.

25　金谷

　　あんたとわたしの想いは一つ
　　忘れもしない ―
　　あんたは夾竹桃(オリアンダー)と　菊(クリサンシマム)の筏のうえ
　　女たちが岸辺でむせび泣く　絹の裳裾を濡らして
　　あんたを遠江(とおとうみ)から
　　わたしの深みに引き込んだ
　　二人で一緒に横たわると
　　やっとあんたは　わたしのもの

　　わたしは名残りの川
　　忘れはしない

【大井川を挟む二つの図】
　島田宿と金谷宿は大井川を挟む。「箱根八里は馬でも越すが、越すに越されぬ大井川」と唄われたように、大井川は水の難所で、ひとたび水かさが増せば川留めとなり、何日も滞留しなければならなかった。この大河の徒渡(かちわた)りの様子を、「島田」では東岸から川越する様子が、「金谷」では大井川を渡り終え、金谷宿のある西岸に向かっている様子が、俯瞰図の連作で描かれている。

26 Nissaka

東海道五拾三次之内　日坂・佐夜ノ中山

    She follows the road, it lists above bamboo,
    tea plantations, mist and blue mountains.

    Every stone covered in moss,
    left-over rain drips,
    pools. Knit one
    purl one. Smell of rotting.

    Sound of branches breaking
    in the wood dense with cryptomeria
    dark as woad.

                Who's there?

    Thwack of blade
    and blood scythes
    from the wound, black rain
    streams, covers
    tree and stone.

    Bamboo and tea trees witness
    a birth and a death,
    say nothing.

    An owl with one eye open
    sighs, heads fall.

            I am wanting to speak to my mother
            but my mother is dead

    The hills sag in bewilderment.

            I am looking for my mother
            but she has disappeared
            I mourn my mother
            from the day I am born

* The print's subtitle is 'Sayo amid the mountains'. The legend tells of a birth at night. At this spot a robber attacked and killed a pregnant woman who had stopped to rest against a stone. A passing Buddhist monk rescued the newborn child. Years later, the murderer took his sword to be mended, boasting to the swordsmith about how he had killed the woman and damaged his sword. The swordsmith, the murdered woman's son, took his revenge. The ghost of the woman lives in the stone; it wails each night.

26　日坂*

　　　女は峠にさしかかる　竹やぶ　茶畑
　　　霧　青き山々のなか

　　　苔むした岩
　　　雫が滴り
　　　水がたまる　一目ずつ
　　　表と裏を編むように　朽ちゆく臭い

　　　枝が折れる音
　　　大青のように杉が生い茂る
　　　暗い森で

　　　　　　そこにいるのは誰？

　　　刃の一振り
　　　血塗られた大鎌
　　　傷口から　黒い雨が
　　　流れだし
　　　木も石も覆い尽くす

　　　竹も茶木も視ていた
　　　一つの生と　一つの死を
　　　何も語らず

　　　片目をあけた梟が
　　　ため息をつき　うなだれる

　　　　　　語りかけたくも
　　　　　　母はなし

　　　山々はうろたえ　うなだれる

　　　　　　求めども
　　　　　　母はいない
　　　　　　母を悼み悲しむ　わたし
　　　　　　生まれ落ちたその瞬間から

原注
＊この版画には「佐夜の中山」という副題がついている。「夜泣き石」の伝説によれば、むかしこの地で、夜に石にもたれて休んでいた妊婦が山賊に襲われて殺された。赤子は通りかかった僧に助けられた。年月が流れ、その盗賊が刀の修理に刀鍛冶にやってきて、刀の刃こぼれは女を殺した時にできたものと自慢した。刀鍛冶は殺された妊婦の息子であり、復讐を果たした。女の霊がこの石に宿って、夜な夜なすすり泣くという。

訳注
大青＝ホソバタイセイ、(葉にインディゴ（藍色）を含み、青色顔料になる)

27 Kakegawa

東海道五拾三次之内　掛川・秋葉山遠望

High-flying kite breaks
through the edge,
lift greater than weight,
silk and bamboo held
by an invisible hand
and pushed upward

Women stoop in a row of nnnnns,
the mud sucks them down,
they plunge on,
insert the shoots one by one
before blue water hems them in

A child stands with wind
at his back,
unreels string
oops! another kite
escapes the frame,
wind takes it over Mt Akiba,
tengu smiles

Five figures on the bridge
hold onto their hats,
lean into it

A day so beautiful
feels like an absence

That's May for you
everything still
within reach

27 掛川

高く舞い上がった凧が
画面の外にとびだす
重力に逆らって
見えない手に操られ
絹糸と竹ひごは
上へ上へと 押し上げられていく

「N」字になって並んだ女たちが
泥に吸い込まれ
泥に突き進み
苗を植える 一本ずつ
やがて青い水が苗をとりまく

子どもが立っている
風を背に
凧紐を繰り出しながら
おっと！ ― もうひとつの凧が
画から飛び出し
秋葉山へと風に運ばれる
天狗がにやり

橋の上の五人の人物
菅笠を抑えて
かがみこむ

こんな美しい日に
不在を想う

五月晴れ
まだ手が届く
何もかも

28 Fukuroi

東海道五拾三次之内　袋井・出茶屋ノ図

sits on a plain.

Wayside shelter, June afternoon
tea kettle hangs from tree branch,
water begins to boil.
Travellers stop for a smoke,
a woman stirs the ashes,
desolate and uncomfortable heat.

Perched on a road direction post
wood thrush sings

    kiskadee

        kata kata kee

Outside the picture frame
a garden with seven hundred cherry trees
and the temple of good fortune.
Two benevolent kings guard the gate:
gape-mouthed Agyō heralds
AH for new beginnings,
zip-lipped Ungyō grunts UNH.
Death has the last word always.

Each winter strong winds gather here,
they say it's a good place for kite flying.

28　袋井

広野(ひろの)に座りこむ

街道脇の小屋　六月の午後
薬缶(やかん)が枝からぶら下がり
湯が沸きはじめる
旅人たちはここらで一服
女が灰をかき混ぜる
ふきっさらしのむし暑さ

道しるべに止まって
森のツグミが囀(さえず)る

　　　　　ケスカディー
　　　　　　　　カタ　カタ　キー

画の外には
七百本の桜木の庭園と
福を呼ぶ寺がある
山門には一対の金剛力士が立ち ─
口を開いた阿形(あぎょう)が告げる
アーと発して　始まりのときを
口を閉じた吽形(うんぎょう)は　ウーンと唸(うな)る
死に際の　あのコトバ

冬になると強風が吹いて
凧あげにはもってこいだとさ

29 Mitsuke

東海道五拾三次之内　見附・天竜川図

I

Mariko's reach always exceeded her grasp,
she couldn't get him
out of her mind. Sure
she got out of bed each morning,
boiled rice, tea,
tried to eat, drink.
Rice stuck in her craw,
she looked in the mirror,
a pelican looked back.
She started to lose weight,
hair, other maiko
kept their distance.
Her insides felt like soba,
nothing connected,
the lump in her throat
moved to her belly.
Hiro didn't return.

II

Two boats moor on a sandy bank,
distant shore draped in mist.
Down-at-the-mouth tour guide
waits with his group,
no glimpse of Fuji today.
Heavenly Dragon River sulks,
chatters with the ferryman.

It's time. Come on
in, the water's fine.

Ahead, Hiro accompanies the sun,
swallows the blame.

29　見附

I
どんなに求めても
いつもマリコからすり抜けた
忘れようにも
忘れられない — そう
朝に床からはい出し
飯を炊き　茶をいれた
口に運び　飲み込もうすると
飯が喉につまった
鏡を覗きこむと
ペリカンが覗き返した
痩せて髪も抜け　まいこたちからも
敬遠され
五臓六腑が蕎麦みたいに
ブツブツと切れた
喉につかえた塊が
腹のほうにおりていく
ヒロは戻ってこなかった

II
渡し船が二艘　砂地に舫う
遠くの岸はかすんで見えない
ご機嫌斜めのツアーガイドが
団体さんと待っている
富士はちらりとも見えない
天竜川 — 天を翔る龍の川 — も不機嫌で
船頭とおしゃべり

　　ぼちぼち　行こうか
　　水かさもいい塩梅だ

ヒロは太陽を道連れに　先を行く
責め苦を呑み込みながら

30 Hamamatsu

東海道五拾三次之内　浜松・冬枯ノ図

Pine trunk draws a line
down the middle of the print,
halfway mark between Edo and Kyoto.

It's not random
but kind of nearly random
Tokaido, life in miniature.

Man with the pipe stands
apart, smoke funnels
round flame.

Four carriers rub their hands
by the fire, so many selves
unspoken

    I am the father flying the kite on my first son's birth,

    I am the monk entering the cave to search,

    I am the kago bearer raising the arms that hold,

    I am the traveller nearing the end of the road.

30　浜松

　　松の幹が真っすぐに
　　画の真ん中に線を引き
　　江戸と京都を二つにわける

　　無作為ではないが
　　ほとんど無作為の
　　東海道　人生の縮図

　　ちょっと離れて
　　キセルをくわえた男が立っている
　　煙が漏斗(じょうご)のように炎から立ちのぼる

　　雲助が四人
　　たき火のそばで手をこする　人生いろいろ
　　口には出さないが

　　　　おれは　総領息子の誕生をいわって凧を挙げる親父

　　　　われは　洞穴で修行する坊主

　　　　おいらは　この腕持ち上げて担ぐ駕篭担き

　　　　われは　旅も終わりの旅人

訳注
雲助＝街道の宿場や渡し場などで、荷物の運搬や駕籠かきなどを仕事としていた無宿の者

【浜松・冬枯ノ図】
　浜松宿は、東海道五十三次の江戸から数えて29番目、京から数えて25番目にあたり、実距離では、江戸から京までのちょうど中間にあたる。それを示すかのように大きな一本松と天へと伸びる焚き火の煙が画面を二分するような大胆な構図がとられている。遠方には、徳川家康が29歳から45歳まで居城していた浜松城が描かれている。

31 Maisaka

東海道五拾三次之内　舞阪・今切真景

Sea and lake now cut

Edges singe as water changes
from indigo to orange.
I emerge in morning light
resolved
to stand up to this place.

The sea dissolves to a lighter
hue, beneath the water
a shoal of fish,
synchronicity.
I feel them sluice
through my veins,
they ply me with sweets

      Open wide
I do.
The creatures in this place
talk in tongues.

I eavesdrop on their conversations
pick up the odd word
or two
    abunai
    gaijin
    da!
I'll take each title
and tell my own story.

31　舞阪

今はもう　海と湖は途切れ

海面(あい)が藍から橙(だいだい)にかわるにつれて
画のふちが赤く焦げる
わたしは　朝の光のなかで
決然と
向かい立つ　この場所に

海のいろは　明るく溶け
海のしたには
魚の群れ
一斉に
群が　わたしの血管に
流れこみ
甘きものを勧める

　　　お口を大きくあけてごらん
あけましょう

生き物たちが　口々に
訳のわからないことばを話す

そのおしゃべりを　盗み聞きして
おもしろいことばを拾い上げる
一つ二つと

　　　危ない
　　　外人
　　　だ！

ひとつひとつのコトバから
わたしの話を紡ぎましょう

【今切とは】
　今切とは静岡県の浜名湖が海に通じるあたりの呼称。1498年の地震で砂州が切れ、遠州灘と浜名湖が繋がって、汽水湖となった。決壊したあたりが今切(いまぎれ)と呼ばれている。

32 Arai

東海道五拾三次之内　荒井・渡舟ノ図

We reach the barrier at midsummer.
Day of the Ox, time to eat eels,
to endure the blaze of August.

Watching him doze on the end of the punt,
more than anything I want to interrupt
his sleep, to fish him from his dream.
I dip my hand in brackish water,
extract an oyster. He sucks out
the sweet flesh in a single gulp.

I lie on tatami watching the sun gild the mist,
the lake comes like a wave.
Most of all I long for your hands
as you wake me from sleep
touching my breasts, my belly,
that tiny pearl, too delicate
for daylight.

Now no one comes
to my bed. I rest my muzzle
against glass until the scene
blurs. Each year at the Day of the Ox
I return to the place where we met.

No one can tell me where this will end.

32　荒井

　　真夏に　関に着く
　　丑の日にはウナギを食べる
　　八月の暑気払い

　　舟の端で居眠りをする男を見ると
　　たまらなく　眠りを削いで
　　夢から釣りあげてみたくなる
　　黒い水に片手を浸して
　　牡蠣をもぎとると　男は
　　その芳醇の身を吸って　ゴクンと呑み込む

　　畳のうえに転がって
　　日差しがもやを金色に染めるのを見ている
　　波のように　湖が寄せてくる
　　何よりも　あなたの手を待ちわびる
　　わたしを目覚めさせて
　　この胸や腹に　この小さな真珠に触れるの
　　陽の光にさらされたら　たちまち壊れてしまうものに

　　今ではもう　訪れるひともない
　　わたしの寝床に　ガラス窓に鼻面をすり寄せて
　　待つの　景色がぼやけていくまで
　　毎年　丑の日に
　　二人が出会った場所に戻る

　　どこまで行けば　終るのか　誰も教えてくれない

【土用丑のうなぎについて】
　図は、舞阪から浜名湖を横切って荒井（新井）宿を目指す「今切の渡し」である。浜名湖は現在ではウナギの養殖で有名であるが、「土用丑の日」に鰻を食べる習慣は江戸時代に作られたようである。もともと、夏の土用は1年で最も暑さが厳しい時期であるため、梅干しやうりなど「う」のつくものを食べると病気をしないとされていた。

33 Shirasuka

東海道五拾三次之内　白須賀・汐見阪図

    Someone has removed
    all the dustbins
    ash heaps
    and excrement.

Pine branches balance the left and right sides, the eye of the observer trails down the slope toward the middle of the print. From right to left a procession leads into the valley. The picture divides neatly into two: all the greenery and human interest in the foreground, broad and open expanse of sea, immaculate beach behind. Feudal lords dressed for travel form another element of the landscape. Walking hats, no face, they represent themselves by shape.

Who is making? Who is speaking? I shuffle crab-like across the surface, lamenting my poor facility with Japanese. Who is Hiro? A painter? A lover? Whose time does he inhabit? And the women who love him? His is a history with no regret.

    Seduced by travel
    Hats process down the hillside

    Lines run out of time

33. 白須賀

　　　みんな片付けてしまったのね
　　　ごみためも
　　　灰の山も
　　　糞尿も　すべて

　松の枝が左右のバランスをとり、見るものの視線が坂を下って画の中央に落ちていく。右から左へと行列が谷に下る。画は、巧みに二分割される ── 前景には植物や人間の趣向のすべてが、背景には、広々とした海と真っ白な砂浜。旅装束(たびしょうぞく)の大名たちがもう一つの景色を創る。歩く笠たち、顔がない、あるのはただ輪郭だけ。

　誰なの？　話しているのは誰？　下手な日本語を嘆きながら、わたしは蟹のように、のろのろと画の表面を横切る。ヒロとは誰？絵師？恋人？彼は誰の時間を生きたの？彼を愛した女たちの時間？それは悔いのない一つの歴史。

　　　旅に　魅せられて
　　　笠たちが　岡の辺を下り

　　　行列が　時を駆け抜けていく

【白須賀宿について】
　白州賀宿はもともと海岸近くにあったが、宝永4年(1707)に発生した地震と津波により大半の家が流されたため、翌年に汐見坂の上に所替えをした。そのため、汐見坂は遠州灘を見渡すことのできる街道一の景勝地となった。図はその絶景を見ながら、大名行列が坂を下っていく様子が描かれている。

34 Futakawa

東海道五拾三次之内　二川・猿ヶ馬場

Two bright sparks pass stone jizō
dressed in a red bib.
Ahead a tea house and sweetness
wrapped in oak leaf,
fare for the passage to Sanjūsangendō
and its thousand Buddhas,
each with forty arms to hold you.

That girl digging in the dirt is me.
She pulls herself apart one section
at a time till she is broken
free. A bad-luck year,
thirty-three for women.
Of all the stations on the old Tokaido
this is the bleakest.

What I dreamed of always was this road.

34 二川

　　二本の閃光が
　　赤いよだれかけの石地蔵を　通りすぎ
　　前方には茶屋
　　柏の葉に包んだ甘きもの
　　三十三間堂の千体仏への旅の糧
　　四十本の腕をもつ仏たちが
　　あなたを抱きしめてくれる

　　土を掘っている少女が　わたし
　　少女は　その身を引き千切る
　　一つ　また一つと　壊れて　自由になるまで
　　女の厄年は
　　三十三歳
　　いにしえの東海道の宿場のうちで
　　ここが　一番わびしい

　　いつもこの道を　夢みていた

訳注
三十三間堂＝京都市東山区の蓮華王院本堂のこと。国宝の本堂三十三間堂の中に千体仏（千手観音立像）がある。

【二川宿について】
　図の左に柏餅をうる茶店が描かれているように、二川は柏餅が名物であった。柏の葉は、上代から食べ物や供物を盛る器として使われおり、新芽が育つまでは古い葉が落ちないことから、「家系が途切れない」「子孫繁栄」という縁起をかついだ。
　三人の女性は、瞽女（ごぜ）と呼ばれる、三味線や唄、踊りなどをして生計を立てていた盲目の旅芸人である。

35 Yoshida

東海道五拾三次之内　吉田・豊川橋

Even in my sleep
the river is always there,
river after river
takes shape,
herds us like cattle
across the flood plain.

So many souls
hide their hurt in the hold,
folded into the rift
between marl and flow.
I see them veiled
in blue membrane
and swimming for the surface
plummy, overripe.

Fear drains into my pillow.
Sometime before dawn
my bed settles into river,
shudder of shingle
fast returns the tide
a few more breaths
and I am lost
to tide-flow.

Grim freight tomorrow
in the crook of the river.

35　吉田

眠っていても
いつも　川がそこにある
川また川が
あらわれてきて
家畜のように群れさせる
氾濫原の向こうに

おびただしい魂たちは
その傷を　船底に隠す
泥と流れの裂け目に
畳まれて
わたしには見える
青い膜におおわれた魂たちが
水面めざして泳いでくる
ぷっくり膨れて　盛りを過ぎて

怖れが　枕に流れ込み
ときには　夜明けまえに
寝床が川の中にすべり込んでいく
板葺き屋根の震え
たちまち　汐が戻る
あとひと息で
汐の流れに
呑み込まれる

明日は　不気味な積荷があがるだろう
川の大曲(おおまがり)で

訳注
大曲＝豊川にかかっている豊川橋（吉田大橋）あたりで、川が直角に曲がっているところ

36 Goyu

東海道五拾三次之内　御油・旅人留女

Kikuyo stands at the window
holding her chin up,

she gazes out at the street
ignoring the punters' cries for help.

Inside a room of nuptial paulownia
Obasan washes someone's feet,

a flight of stairs with drawers in the risers
leads nowhere.

A kitchen with a deal table
holds all matter of things –

leeks, laver, a bulbous
daikon, fragrance of fermenting.

Remove your sentiments
and leave them outside the door.

You are never more at home
than when you are here.

36　御油

　　　キクヨは窓辺に立つ
　　　あごをつきあげて

　　　通りを見つめる
　　　助けをもとめる客の声など気にも留めず

　　　旅籠の中は　婚礼の桐の間
　　　おばさんが客の足を洗う

　　　階段箪笥の先は
　　　どこへも続かない

　　　白木の配膳台がある台所には
　　　いろんなものが処狭し

　　　ニラに　アオサに　丸大根
　　　糠床の臭い

　　　感傷なんか
　　　外に捨てておいで

　　　ここにいるのが
　　　いちばん寛ぐんだから

訳注
白木の配膳台＝deal table は楡材や松材の白木の厚版

【留女について】
　副題の留女とは旅籠の客引きのことであるが、夜は飯盛り女としても働いた。御油と次の赤阪は1.7キロメートルの近さで、両宿場とも飯盛り女が多く、二つの図を見ることで当時の旅籠の様子が見えてくる。本図は夕暮れ時の様子である。客を引っ張り込もうとする留女と強引に掴まえられている旅人たち、その様子を窓辺で平然とみている女、そして、宿に引き込まれ足を洗う旅人。街道でのこの一場面を、遠近法の描写が一層浮きたたせている。

37 Akasaka

東海道五拾三次之内　赤坂・旅舎招婦ノ図

There is always a river, a lake, the sea: a crossing through water, over a bridge, a tortured pine sometimes covered in snow. A road, setting out, places abandoned. Some remembered.

Wandering and observing the landscape, travellers follow a route, encounter obstacles, make choices, progress.

This time however the artist foregrounds a sago palm in the courtyard. It just fits. An interior scene, doors open. A cupboard stacked with futon. Black hair drifts.

Geisha apply their make-up, a man returns from his bath. A pair of legs descends the stairs.

Give me your hand and
I will be
anything you want.

37　赤坂

　　いつも川があり　湖があり　海がある ― 川を渡り
　　橋を越える　ときに　曲がりくねった松は雪景色　一本の街道
　　旅に出て　捨てられる場所もあり　忘れられない場所もある

　　彷徨い　景色を眺め　旅人たちは街道をゆく
　　行きづまり　選びとり　進んでゆく

　　でもこんどは　中庭の前景に　絵師が大きなソテツを描く
　　ぴったりだ　家の中が窺える　ふすまが開いている　布団を詰め込んだ
　　押し入れ　黒髪が流れる

　　芸者は化粧し　男は風呂から戻る
　　二本の足が階段を下りてくる

　　　　さあ　あたいの手をとって
　　　　好きなように
　　　　しておくれ

訳注
二本の足が階段を下りてくる＝「二本の足」で男の客を表している。修辞法の換喩の手法。

【旅籠について】
　旅籠は旅の疲れを癒す。入浴、食事、あん摩、飯盛女との戯れ ― この一図がそれらすべての様子を見せる。赤坂には東海道筋で最後まで営業を続けた旅籠として有名な「大橋屋」があったが、2015年3月15日に営業を終了した。図に描かれたソテツは現在、近くの寺院に移植されているらしい。

38 Fujikawa

東海道五拾三次之内　藤川・棒鼻ノ図

Outside town a ferryman with a blue
tattoo squats in a hedge of ajisai.
He bends over to pick one,
cartwheels through the door
and lands on the floor,
Thud. The future only half-assured.

July has only begun, and already
the fields have changed to amber.

Like the others I sit with my legs folded
under, forehead bang-on-brick.
The cramp starts in the arch,
writhes upwards and emerges
in wet mascara. I try flattery
till eventually the foot goes numb,
hangs there like blancmange.

Even the cats have bowed down for the shōgun.
No one notices
the artist rendered there.

38 藤川

　　　宿場のはずれで　青い刺青の渡し守が
　　　紫陽花の垣根にうずくまり
　　　一枝取ろうと身をかがめて
　　　入り口のほうに転がる　下には土
　　　ドスン
　　　先のことは半分もわからない

　　　7月に入ったばかりなのに
　　　野原はもうこはく色

　　　わたしも真似して　土下座し
　　　額を　下へ下へと　すりつける
　　　土ふまずが　痙攣
　　　身をよじると　上へ上へと
　　　ついにマスカラが濡れる　その場をなんとかごまかしたが
　　　やがて足も痺れ
　　　ブラマンジェのようにぶら下がる

　　　猫も将軍に頭を下げる
　　　誰も気づかないだろうね
　　　そこに絵師がいたことに

訳注
ブラマンジェ＝フランス語のブラン・マンジェ（白い食べもの）。プリンのような冷菓の一つ。

【藤川・棒鼻ノ図】
　この図は、毎年8月1日に江戸幕府が京都の朝廷に馬を献上する行事「八朔御馬進献」の行列が描かれたものとされている。二頭の献上馬に御幣が立てられ、宿場役人たちが棒鼻まで一行を土下座して出迎えている様子である。広重は天保3年（1832）にこの行列に参加した。

39 Okazaki

東海道五拾三次之内　岡崎・矢矧之橋

Many crossings, sometimes a bridge. Edge-to-edge, the longest bridge on the Tokaido. Water showcases girders. The eye level with the hills. A procession passes bearing a crest with 38 ravens surrounding an equal number of out-facing arrows. Everyone is going to Okazaki Castle.

In Egypt the pharaohs were laid to rest with 38 cat guardians, 38 ankhs. In 1888 a clowder of 300,000 mummified cats was discovered, ground up and sent to England to be used as fertiliser. The Egyptians killed whoever put a cat to death.

If I had only stayed in Japan. But I wanted to grab the world by the scruff before my neck turned to crepe. Road-struck. Because it could take me somewhere. Different, but never home.

Mariko removed the mote from my eye. Like an amulet I carried her. In the desert her star shone bright. The river bore the pretty worm that kills. I lick my skin to get rid of the smell of the place.

39　岡崎

ほとんどが渡しだが、ときには橋がある。端から端を測ると東海道の最長の橋。水に映る見事な橋桁。目線のあたりに丘があり、大名行列が通り過ぎる。外向きにつけられた 38 の矢羽根の周りに 38 枚の大鴉の羽をつけた毛槍を先頭に、一行は岡崎城へと向かう。

エジプトでは、ファラオは 38 匹の猫の守護神と 38 のアンサタ十字とともに埋葬された。1888 年に 30 万匹の猫のミイラ群が発見され、粉末にしてイギリスに送られ、肥料にされた。エジプト人は猫を殺した者を、誰かれ構わず死刑に処した。

日本にとどまっていさえしたら！でも、首がチリメンのようにシワだらけになる前に、世界のなんたるかを掴み取りたかったの。道に魅せられて。もしかしたら、どこかに連れて行ってくれるかもしれない道だったから。どこか違う場所に。でも、ふるさとに向かう道ではなかった。

マリコがわたしの目を覚ましてくれたの。お守りのように、彼女を連れ歩いたわ。砂漠ではマリコの星が明るく輝き、川にはキレイな毒虫がいた。場所の匂いを消すために、自分の皮膚を舐めるわたし。

訳注
橋＝矢作橋。徳川時代の日本最長の橋。
アンサタ十字＝上に輪がついて十字架。古代エジプトで生命の象徴。

40 Chiryū

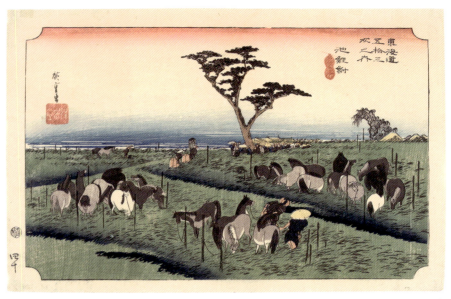

東海道五拾三次之内　池鯉鮒・首夏馬市

April, the pasture flows
with long grass and horses.
Why can't we go on like this for ever?

Horses prick up their ears, invent
their next journey,
how it will change things.

Those men colluding under the tree
mean nothing, I yearn for the sea
today coated in quicksilver.

Each of us has a price
on our heads, we are not the same
as when we started all those rivers ago.

The sea brings armfuls of dulse,
a prospect that whatever happens to others
needn't happen to me. Forget

November's darkening tale,
leap into seafoam. It's a day for wading
through waves, for swimming until myself ceases.

40　池鯉鮒

　　四月は　草原に
　　丈の高い草や馬たちが溢れる　一体どうして
　　いつまでも　こんな風に生きていられないのだろう

　　馬たちは耳をそばだて
　　次の旅を思い描く
　　どんな暮らしが待っているのだろう

　　樹の下で談合する男たちなど
　　どうでもいい　今日は
　　鈍色(にびいろ)の海に　心惹かれる

　　みんな頭に値札をつけて旅しているが
　　いくつもの橋を渡り始めたあの頃の
　　ままではないだろう

　　海は抱えきれないほどの紅藻(ダルス)を運んでくるけれど
　　人に起こることが何でもわたしに起こるとは限らない　なんて
　　期待するのは　やめましょう

　　十一月の黄昏どきのおはなし　海の泡に一飛び
　　波間をぬって歩くには　もってこいの日
　　命果てるまで泳いでいくには　もってこいの日

【首夏馬市について】
　首夏馬市は、陰暦4月の25日から5月5日にかけて、宿場のはずれでおこなわれた大規模な馬市。中央の松は、この周辺で馬主や仲買人が馬の値段を決めたことから「談合松」と呼ばれている。地名の池鯉鮒は、現在は「知立」と書く。

41 Narumi

東海道五拾三次之内　鳴海・名物有松絞

Down the bank, reeds uncouple,
Hiro disappears like a flame in sunlight.

Kikuyo stays behind, curled into a round ball,
Licking her wounds.

•

Cloth ripples, scene changes.
Arimatsu. Trays arrayed
with storm shibori
blue beyond blue.
Long after you
these hold the shape, scent
of you, until a great wind comes
and irons out the creases.

Roused by the lap of a wave,
the promise of a river,
so many crossings,
you can't remember
all that has happened.
Yes, you've come that far.

41　鳴海

土手をくだると　葦が分かれ
ヒロは　陽光のなかの炎のように　姿を消す

キクヨは後にとどまり　丸い玉のように身を丸めて
傷口を舐める

●

布が波うち　場面が変わる
有松　あらし絞りの盆がずらり
どこまでも藍
遠く離れても
あなたの姿と残り香がまだここにある
大風が来て
縮みのひだを
すっかり伸ばしてしまうまで

ヒタヒタと押し寄せる波が
川の約束を呼びおこす
たくさんの川を渡ってきたのに
もう　あなたには思い出せない
二人の過去のすべてが
そう ― あなたはこんなに遠くまで来てしまった

訳注
あらし絞り＝はじめ有松村で生産され、鳴海で販売をあつかった木綿の絞り。有松絞は近代になって新しい手法を取り入れて、あらし絞りと呼ばれる。東海道に面した鳴海宿には多くの絞りの店が軒を連ねた。

42 Miya

東海道五拾三次之内　宮・熱田神事

A horse and men chasing it.
Perpendicular lines on the right
suggest a shrine at festival time.

All the action takes place
in the centre of the field.
Under a piebald sky the men abandon

themselves to tug-of-war.
I enter their world,
play the game.

Parallel plumes of smoke
rise from the corner,
women shelter

behind wood and silk.
The naked one absorbs
bad luck and evil deeds.

I breathe in the brume.
The men pull back, surge through,
Noli me tangere.

Enter the frame and you're tempted to stay,
too long and you fray the boundary
between semblance and reality.

If you are lucky you will penetrate the place,
lay your hands on the sword of billowing clouds,
though it will not bring you joy.

I'm part of this now.
Follow me to the bridge, I'll show you
the way out.

42　宮

　　　　人馬がソレを追う
　　　　右手に垂直線がそびえ
　　　　宮のお祭りらしい

　　　　行事はすべて
　　　　境内の中央で
　　　　むら雲の空の下　男たちが

　　　　綱引きに興じる
　　　　わたしもその世界に飛び込んで
　　　　競い合いに興じる

　　　　綿毛のような二筋の煙の柱が
　　　　隅からたちのぼり
　　　　女たちは　木と絹の後ろに

　　　　身を隠す
　　　　裸男は　凶運と厄運を
　　　　吸いこみ

　　　　わたしは　もやを　吸う
　　　　男たちは　引いては　押し寄せる
　　　　ノリ　メ　タンゲレ

　　　　画のなかに入れば　そこに居たくなり
　　　　長くとどまれば　外と内の境目が
　　　　ほつれていく

　　　　運がよければ　ここに入り込んで
　　　　まきあがる雲の剣に　その手で　触れられるかも
　　　　喜びというほどではないにしても

　　　　わたしはもう　その一部
　　　　橋のところまで　ついておいで
　　　　教えてあげる　ここからの出口を

訳注
ノリ　メ　タンゲレ＝（ラテン語）「我に触れるな」、復活したイエスのマグダラのマリアへの言葉（ヨハネよる福音書20-17）。
雲の剣＝日本神話の天の叢雲の劔。三種の神器の一つの「草薙の劔」あるいは「天叢雲の劔」。倭姫尊から賜ったこの劔で、日本武尊が草をなぎ切って、難を逃れたのが由来。熱田神宮の神宝。

　【宮宿について】
　　宮とは熱田神宮のことである。熱田宿とも呼ばれ、古くから熱田神宮の門前町として栄え、次の桑名宿とは七里の渡しで結ばれていた。図は、熱田で端午に行われていた「馬の塔」と呼ばれる神事で、豪華な馬具で飾った馬を社寺へ奉納する様子である。赤い半纏と青い半纏を着た男たちが列をなして駆けてゆく姿に、勢いとスピードが感じられる。

43 Kuwana

東海道五拾三次之内　桑名・七里渡口

I look for the golden flame
on the bank of the Kiso River.
The boat takes us
to a tea house,
wooden floors polished
by repetitions.

Here the sake tastes of flowers,
over the ayu
we put our differences aside.

I look for you in a poem
but find only unendingness,
imagine a day so light
even memories float away.

I look at your name written on card
in your own hand, the number I call
and call but no one ever picks up.

43　桑名

　　　わたしは　金色の炎を探す
　　　木曽川の岸で
　　　小舟が二人を
　　　茶屋に連れてゆく
　　　木の床がつやつやと光っている
　　　繰り返し踏まれて

　　　さあ　花の香りの酒をどうぞ
　　　鮎を肴に
　　　すれ違いなど　しばし忘れて

　　　わたしは　詩のなかに　あなたを探す
　　　でも　見つけたのは　果てしなさだけ
　　　あんまり微かな一日だったので
　　　思い出さえもふわふわと逃げていく

　　　あなたの名前を見つめる
　　　あなたの手書きの名刺　何度も　何度もかけた電話番号
　　　でも　誰も出ない

【七里の渡について】
　宮宿と桑名宿は「七里の渡し」と呼ばれる海路で結ばれる。所要時間は４時間程度で、その間足を休めることができちょうどよい旅の休息であったようだ。桑名は、木曽川・揖斐川・長良川の三河川が落ち合う水郷の町として、物資流通の中継点となり産業が栄えた。「その手は桑名の焼き蛤」(その手は食わない、というしゃれ)と言われるように、桑名は焼き蛤が名物で、それを食べるのも旅の楽しみであった。図は揖斐川河口にある桑名の渡し口近くに到着したところである。船着き場には伊勢神宮の一の鳥居が立っており、伊勢参りの玄関口であった。現在でも、式年遷宮ごとに伊勢神宮宇治橋の鳥居を移して建て替えられている。

44 Yokkaichi

東海道五拾三次之内　四日市・三重川

I bring myself back to the picture –
a willow anchors the centre
a hat rolls along the jetty
a man chasing it;
soon it will fall out of the frame
(bottom left). My eye shunts to a figure,
arms pinioned, his cloak billows
against a sky of zinc.

This is a good place to die.
I have brought myself back across decades.
Upriver little boats moor amongst benevolent reeds,
news bulletins warn of the coming storm.
Some take heed but there's always a fool
who stands on a jetty facing it.
Take me, I'm yours.

44 Yokkaichi

I thought I had finished with the little
danchi on the plain, but I bring myself back,
leaning into the head wind
to get inside. We unrolled
the day, drank absinthe under glass
marked 'X'. It was nice
like a holiday, bunking off.
Even when the hurricane's eye
spied our bed we felt safe
from the peril
ten years ahead.

I reach out to touch you and darkness bleeds
from my fingertips. Never would I have
thought to return here
but I bring myself back
to the same street on the same date
and someone I have never met
opens the door. I catch
a glimpse of an old woman
in the mirror at his back.

44　四日市

　　もういちど　画に戻ってくる —
　　中央に柳が一本　碇を下ろし
　　笠が船着場を転がっていく
　　男がそれを追いかける —
　　ああ — 笠が画から転がり落ちそう
　　(画面左下) 目をそらすと　人影
　　両腕を丸め込み　外套を風にはためかせて
　　青白い空を背に

　　死ぬにはもってこいの場所ね
　　戻ってきたのよ　何十年の歳月を超えて
　　川上の　慈悲深い葦間には　小舟が舫い
　　ニュースが　嵐の到来を告げる
　　警戒するものもいれば
　　風に抗って船着場に立つ　阿呆もいる
　　わたしを連れて行って　わたしはあなたのものだから

44　四日市

　　　平地での狭い団地暮らしはもうやめようと思ったけれど
　　　でも戻ってくるの
　　　向かい風に身をかがめて
　　　中に入っていく　あの日をひもときながら
　　　二人でアブサンを飲んだわ
　　　底に「X」と書かれたコップで
　　　素敵だったわ　まるで休日みたいに　サボったりして
　　　ハリケーンの目に
　　　寝床を覗かれても
　　　危険なんてないと感じたわ
　　　10年先までだって

　　　手を伸ばしてあなたに触れる　闇が
　　　指先から流れ出す　思いもしなかったわ
　　　ここに戻るなんて
　　　でも　わたしは戻った
　　　同じ街に　同じ日に
　　　そして　見知らぬ誰かが
　　　ドアを開けるの
　　　老婆がちらりと見えたわ
　　　男の背中の鏡のなかに

訳注
死ぬにはもってこいの場所＝アメリカインディアンの警句、「今日は死ぬにはもってこいの日だ」（タオス・プエブロの古老の言葉）を想起させる表現。

【四日市宿について】
　四日市は、現在はコンビナートのある工業地帯として有名であるが、かつては三重川（現在は三滝川）の河口の湊町だった。宮宿と桑名宿が「７里の渡し」で結ばれていたように、少し南に位置する四日市宿とは「１０里の渡し」があった。宿場の南には、東海道から分岐する伊勢参宮道の起点である日永の追分があり、旅人はここから伊勢神宮を目指した。
　図の中の、合羽の裾が風に吹き上げられる旅人、その反対方向に行く旅人、強い風で揺れる柳ら、これらは旅のもの寂しさや人生の辛さを語っている。一方で、笠を飛ばされ必死につんのめるように追う男が滑稽である。

45 Ishiyakushi

東海道五拾三次之内　石薬師・石薬師寺

Yakushi Buddha
holds his right hand in mudra,
sun and moon, his caretakers.

In the canopy crickets sing
a lament of summer's passing.
Sun going down backlights mountain,
birds ribbon lapis-lazuli sky.

Garbed in grey I anchor
on the bank of a shallow river,
an egret settles next to me.
We both stare ahead,
always travellers
in a foreign place.

Those we've left never change.

We talk until the belling
of a temple returns through trees.
*When it comes to leaving
you birds are the experts.*
Egrets scatter like leaves.

At Ishiyakushi, Buddha of Healing
tells you not to fear.

Moon sweeps the path clean.

45　石薬師

薬師如来が
右手で印を結ぶ
日光と月光が　その脇侍(わきじ)

天蓋のなかで　コオロギが鳴く
過ぎゆく夏を惜しんで
山の端を赤く染めながら　太陽が沈む
鳥たちが瑠璃色の空を　リボンのように飛んでいく

灰色の衣に身を包み　わたしは
浅瀬の土手に　腰を下ろす
シラサギが　隣に来てとまる
いっしょに前方を見つめる
あいもかわらず　旅人ばかり
見知らぬ土地には

別れた人は　いつまでも変わらない

寺の鐘の音が　木の間にこだまして戻るまで
二人で語り合う
別れのこととなると
鳥たちの　見事なこと
シラサギが木の葉のように散っていく

石薬師で　薬師如来が語りかける
恐れるなかれと

月が清らかに道を照らす

【石薬師寺について】
　宿名となっている石薬師寺（三重県鈴鹿市）は、弘法大使空海が石に線刻したと伝えられる薬師如来を本尊としている。刻まれている如来像は、右手を胸の前に挙げて掌を前に向け、「恐れなくてよい」を意味する施無畏印(せむいいん)のポーズをとる。参勤交代の大名も立ち寄り、ここで道中の安全祈願をした。

46 Shōno

東海道五拾三次之内　庄野・白雨

Low cloud confounds the yews,
rain riffles robes,
chimes off stones,
oxidises the mountain
bars on the road.

We had taken a wrong turn.
No one wants to arrive
after dark.

Steam rises from us,
hovers above houses.
Resignation
spills from collars,
trickles down necks,
goads us
on to Tojimbo

Yoisho

      Yoish o

Tree elders topped in grey
watch us run our course.

The stone ahead
becomes the headstone.

46　庄野

低い雲は　イチイの木を惑わす
雨は　キモノの裾をめくり
石にあたって　鐘のように響き
街道の山坂を
燻(いぶ)していく

道を間違ってしまった
日がくれて宿に着きたいと思うものなど
誰もいない

からだから湯気があがり
家々のうえを舞う
諦めが
うなじから　こぼれ
首筋にしたたる
東尋坊まで
急(せ)き立てる

　　　　よいしょ
　　　　　　　　よいし　ょ

白髪頭の　年古(ふ)りた木々が
走りゆくものたちを見つめる

行く手の石が
墓石にかわる

訳注
東尋坊＝福井県北部（坂井市）の海岸にある景勝地。日本海の侵食を受けた輝石安山岩の柱状節理がそそり立つ。自殺の名所。

47 Kameyama

東海道五拾三次之内　亀山・雪晴

No smoke trails from the chimneys,
everyone's asleep. Hiro walks with the howling wind
and fast-flowing clouds to a different world.

A crane with silver wings glances back,
urges him to follow. In Kameyama's yard
many tombs buried in deep snow.

A small party reduced by a grey and mangy sky.
No sound but the travellers' panting and coughing,
they clutch at tufts of wind.

Hiro gutters, out of sorts, mumbles something
disagreeable to his companion;
crane changes course, disappears over trees.

*It would be easy to sink down under a thick fleece
until your last breath shimmers.*

A woman sits alone on a temple porch.
Snow is falling.

47　亀山

家々の煙は落ちて
誰もが眠りにつくころ　ヒロは咽ぶような風と
飛びさる雲とともに　別の世へと歩いていく

銀色の翼の鶴が　振り返りながら　ついておいでとヒロを促す
亀山の野の　深い雪のなかに
おびただしい墓が埋もれている

灰色のくすんだ空に閉ざされた　小さな一団
聞こえるのは　喘ぎと咳払いばかり
風の房をつかみながら　旅人がゆく

ヒロは消え入りそうに　イライラと
不平をもらす ― 不快な繰り言
鶴がコースをかえて　木々の彼方に消えてゆく

　　ふかふかのフリースの下に　沈んでいくのは訳もないこと
　　あなたの最後の息が　微かに光るまで

女が一人　寺の入り口に座っている
雪が降る

【亀山・雪晴】
　亀山は難所の鈴鹿峠をひかえ、隣の関宿と共に栄えた。図の右隅には亀山城があり、急な傾斜を大名行列が連なって登っている。山際の薄紅の光、白い雪、藍の天ぼかしから、良く晴れた冬の朝の景色とされているが、実際にその場所に立ってみると、朝焼けとして描かれている方向は東でなく西に位置する。広重は実際には東海道を歩いていないとよく言われるように、必ずしも事実に忠実というわけではないようである。

48 Seki

東海道五拾三次之内　関・本陣早立

Blue, blue is the sky
indifferent to my pain.
I have travelled far
to see him again,
told he died
last winter.

His ashes mulch the sakura.
I am given a shawl
dyed with their blossoms.
This is not
what I wanted
this is not it
at all.

Why bother to brush my hair?
I'll live out my days
in aimlessness,
close and lock the gate,
let the knotweed take the rest.

48　関

空は　限りなく青い
この身の痛みなど　われ関せずと
はるばると旅をしてきたの
もう一度あの人に会いたくて
誰かが言ったの ―
去年の冬に　あの人はこの世を去ったと

あの人の遺灰は桜の根もとに埋められ
桜の花びらで染めた
肩掛けが残された
こんなもの
欲しくはなかった
こんなもの
なんか

髪を梳(くしけず)るのも疎ましく
ただあてもなく
この日々を生きていく　わたし
門をしめて　鍵をかけ
あとのことは　蓼(たで)にでも任せましょう

訳注
蓼＝英語の'knotweed'は締めつける草のこと。黒魔術で使われる言葉で、人の行動を操ったり支配するものとして使われる。

【関宿について】
　関宿は、東追分から西追分まで約1.8 kmにわたり、東の追分からは伊勢別街道、西の追分からは大和街道が分岐し、東海道を合わせて3街道の分岐点に位置する活気ある宿場町であった。面白いことに、街道沿いの旅籠の看板は、西側（京都側）は漢字で、東側（江戸側）は仮名で書かれていた。これは、京方面に行く場合は「かな」を、江戸方面に行く場合は「漢字」を見ながら歩くことで、方向を間違えないための工夫だと言われている。これで、日の出前の出発でも方向を間違えることがない。図は、早朝大名行列が宿場の本陣から出発する様子である。

49 Sakanoshita

東海道五拾三次之内　坂之下・筆捨嶺

The painter throws his brush
in a fit of pique.
Jun ken po
I cannot show,
mountain wins.

Clear streams cover mossy
stones in cobalt green.
That old fugitive, time
skulks in the shadows,
waits for the brush to fall.

A flock of herons
skein through schist,
scent the sea and know themselves
to be blue water.

Observers at the edge
toss pebbles to judge
where land meets ravine.

Kano Motonobu's ghost
slides through eel grass,
owl in the larches
murmurs *hoooo*

49　坂之下

絵師が筆を投げ捨てる
憤懣(ふんまん)やる方なく
ジャンケンポン
あいこでしょ
「グー（山）」の勝ち

コバルト・グリーンの
澄みきった水が　苔むした石をおおう
あの年老いた逃亡者が
　― 時の闇にひそかに身を隠して ―
筆が投げ捨てられるのを待っている

鷺の群れが
糸枷せように
片岩をまわり
海の匂いをかぎ　やがて紺碧の海となる

崖のうえの眺望者たちは
小石を投げ込んで確かめる
谷底の深さを

狩野元信の亡霊が
アマモのあいだを　ひそかにうごめく
フクロウが　カラマツのなかで
ホ ―― と呟やく

訳注
狩野元信＝（1476-1559）室町後期の画家。漢画様式に土佐派の大和絵の手法を取り入れて、両派の融合を図り、桃山障壁画の狩野派の基礎を築いた。図に描かれている筆捨山は、狩野派二代目の元信が、刻々と変化する山の風景の美しさに感動し、絵を描くのを諦めて筆を捨てたという伝説から名付けられた。
アマモ（eel grass）＝ 海草

50 Tsuchiyama

東海道五拾三次之内　土山・春之雨

The cinereous sky knows the hour
of the sun's setting but isn't saying.

There is a river near here
where she walked one day

filled her pockets with flint
and stepped in.

As if into a lightless room,
she reached out her hands

and grasped the hollowness.
I gather up the liquid of her

last breath into my hands,
and afterwards stand with my back

to the rain, taking its lashings
without once crying out

without crying out once.
The river looks beyond

says, 'Someone will return
to take her place.'

I come away peeling off
the wet garments of grief,

turn my pockets inside out.
Two days later they find her

mangled and silenced
in the pulp of the river.

50. 土山

灰色の空は　日没を知るが
語ろうとはしない

近くに川があり
あるとき　女が歩いていた

ポケットに重い石をつめこんで
水に入っていった

まるで　光のない部屋に入っていくように
女は　両の手を広げて

虚ろを掴んだ ―
わたしは　この両の手のなかに

女の流れる最後の息を　拾い集め
立ち尽くし

雨に背を向けて　その鞭を受けた
ただの一度も　泣き叫ばず

泣き叫んだりせず　ただの一度も ―
川が　かなたを見つめて

語る「誰かが戻ってきて
あの女の代わりになるさ」

わたしは　去っていく
悲しみの濡れ衣を脱ぎ

ポケットをひっくり返して ―
二日の後　女が見つかる

切りきざまれ　物言わぬまま
ドロドロと泥にまみれて

51 Minakuchi

東海道五拾三次之内　水口・名物干瓢

I lie back and try not to think
of August 6, 1945,
rather observe the pine plumes,
the blue hills of Kyoto.

Women sit in the sun peeling gourds
and hanging the ochreous flesh
from scaffolds. The wind blows the door
open, bombs yet to fall.

Winter welters in my blood.
I think I'm on the Sea of Japan,
it's that bitter cold. People interrupt
me – mother's voice: *One must
always think of others first*.
Like her I now wear sensible shoes.

I watch the twig-carriers
making and mending, heard
the cuckoo this morning.

51 水口

横になって 考えないようにするの
1945年8月6日のこと
羽毛のような松の穂や
青い京都の山並みに　目をやって

女たちは　陽だまりで　瓢箪の皮をむき
黄土色の果肉を　柵に吊るす
風が扉をおしあける
爆弾はまだ降ってこない

冬が　血のなかでうねる
きっと　日本海にいるんだわ　わたし
身を刺すように寒い
わたしを遮るものがいる ― 母の声
いつでも人のことを先に考えるのよ
母に倣って　いまはめだたない靴をはく

小枝を運んで
巣作りをしているわ
今朝　郭公が啼いていた

訳注
1945年8月6日＝第二次世界大戦（太平洋戦争）が決着した広島の原爆投下の日

【水口・名物干瓢】
　干瓢は水口の代表的な特産物である。図は、初夏の風物詩である干瓢づくりの風景で、青空の下で、三人の女たちが干瓢の原料となる夕顔の実を細長く切って干しているところである。

52 Ishibe

東海道五拾三次之内　石部・目川ノ里

Night plummets as it does on the plain,
mist ambles through woods.
Only the tips of the mountain, grey
for a while, and the sea in the distance,
stretching its vast empty limbs.
Hiro stands and watches
the colour drain from the day.
Some will make it.
Some won't.

Michi ni mayotte shimaimashita

Then light from an inn trips into the street,
dancers let what comes
go. Others leave the little show,
walk towards the acid blue horizon.

She greets him with a cup of rice wine

It will be a radiant night.

You're just one among many
who vanished.

52　石部

つるべ落としの夜がくる　野に闇が落ちるように
霧が　森をそぞろ歩く
山の端だけが　しばし　薄墨色
遠くの海は
果てしなく　空っぽの手足を広げる
ヒロは立たずんで
昼の色が抜け落ちてゆくのを見つめる
うまくいくものもあり
いかぬもあり

みちにまよってしまいました

宿の明かりが道にながれ
踊る連中が　人を寄せたり　離したり
余興をはなれて　歩き去るものがいる
青色の地平線をめざして

女が　杯をかざして　男を出迎える

華やかな夜になるだろう

あんたも　また
消えていった沢山の人たちの　ひとりなのに

【石部・目川ノ里】
　水口宿を過ぎ草津宿の手前に目川がある。目川は菜飯と豆腐田楽を名物とし、図には、菜飯田楽を食べさせる茶屋で実在した「いせや」が描かれている。店の前には「伊勢踊り」を踊りながら、京から伊勢参りに向かう一団がいる。後ろにはびわ湖、その奥に比良山が見える。

53 Kusatsu

東海道五拾三次之内　草津・名物立場

Mariko misspent her youth
at the inn of The Cat Who Laughed.

Hirata-gumo weaves his web
across the threshold.

*I've been a good girl
gone around the world.*

She stays up all night, lies abed
all day while her lust turns grey.

Hiro waits at the bridge
with something to say.

The camellia he gave her
rises up like onryō,

wind thrashes trees
till leaves submit.

*I am no longer young.
Pain endures.*

Live with it.

111

53　草津

マリコは　青春を棒に振った
あの「笑い猫」の宿で

平蜘蛛（ひらたぐも）が　敷居一面に
巣をかける

わたし　ずっと　いい子だったのよ
世界を経巡（へめぐ）って

一晩中　まんじりともせず　日がな一日
寝床で横になる　やがて　欲望も薄ぼけていく

ヒロが　橋のたもとで待っている
何か　もの言いたげに

あの男（ひと）が女にわたした椿が
怨霊のように立ちのぼる

風が　木々を激しく打つ
葉が散ってしまうまで

もう若くはないの
痛みは続く

それを道連れに　生きていきましょう

54　Ōtsu

東海道五拾三次之内　大津・走井茶店

It is the nature of the river
to divide. Kneeling at the water's edge
I turn over pale stones.

I am almost never here
in these old prints, but look harder,
closer, and I'm everywhere.

I've attenuated each title
entreated each kanji
until it is able to speak

until I begin to dream
in another language
with no word for loss.

54　大津

別れは川の定め
わたしは　水辺にしゃがみ込んで
蒼白い石をめくる

この古い画のなかの　もう　どこにも
わたしはいない　けれど　もっと目をこらすと
どこにでも　わたしがいる

一つひとつの題名を　飾らず
一つひとつの漢字に　祈りを込めてきた
やがて　それが語ることができるようになるまで

異国の　ことばで
夢を　みはじめるまで
一語たりとも　逃すことなく

【大津宿について】
　大津宿は、東海道と北国街道の分岐点にある。北陸などの日本海側の特産物が敦賀や若狭の小浜で陸揚げされた後、琵琶湖水運で大津港まで運びこまれ、それを牛車で京都まで運ぶ。図の街道には三台の牛車が並んで進む。左下には水がこんこんと湧き出ている「走井」と呼ばれる井戸と、その横に湧水で作られた走井餅を売る茶屋がある。京まであと少し。ここで喉を潤し休息を取る。

55 Kyoto

東海道五拾三次之内　京師・三条大橋

At Sanjo Bridge
the hills are swagged in snow,
the river's surface solid,

deceptive. Beneath its weathered
veins a cold current runs
from source to sea.

Temple smoke streams over the bridge,
purifies pilgrims, eyes
fix on the city of dreams.

There is no clear boundary
between memory and imagination,
memory carries a trace

of place, gives us presence
in absence. Imagination
mends the holes.

I let you go, my blue
familiars, cross the bridge
alone.

55　京都

　　三条大橋
　　山々は雪に　たわみ
　　川面は　かたい

　　欺くように　風化したその血脈の下を
　　一筋の冷たい流れが　走る
　　源から海へと

　　橋にただよう　寺の煙に
　　巡礼者は清められ　瞳は
　　夢の都に　釘づけになる

　　記憶と想像の　はざまに
　　はっきりとした　境はない
　　記憶は ─

　　場所の名残を　かかえて
　　不在のなかに存在を蘇らせ　想像は ─
　　ほころびを繕う

　　さあ　行きなさい　わたしの
　　蒼く親しきものたちよ　橋を渡りなさい
　　その身ひとつで

【京師(けいし)・三条大橋】
　「京師」とは「都」のことで、つまり京都のことである。江戸の日本橋を出発して歩き、時には船で川や海を渡ってきた東海道の旅も、終点の三条大橋にたどり着いた。三条大橋には、様々な人々が行き来する ─ 行商人、番傘を指す武士たち、茶筅売り（中央やや右）、欄干から鴨川の流れを見ている人もいる。背景には比叡山、清水山、その麓には古都の街並みが描かれている。

用語集 Glossary

Abunai（アブナイ）＝危険。

Agyo（アギョウ）＝阿形と吽形（の動物）は神社仏閣の守護者。この恐ろしい形相は悪霊を追い払うもので、それぞれの名前は宇宙の音を表している。口を開いた阿形は生（始まりを）を表す音「ア」を示し、口を閉じたもう一方は「ウン」または「オーム」の音を表し、終焉、すなわち死を意味する。〔「オーム」はア・ウ・ムの三音から成る宇宙の聖音〕

Ajisai（アジサイ）＝紫陽花。〔日本では６月に開花する庭木〕

Asa（アサ）＝朝。「朝の富士」あるいは、「モーニング富士」

Ayu（アユ）＝鮎。美味の川魚。

Daikon（ダイコン）＝大根。円柱型の長く白い根菜。

Daimyo（ダイミョウ）＝大名。封建領主。

Danchi（ダンチ）＝団地。1950年から70年代に開発された住宅区域、集合的なアパート住宅群。

Dharma（ダルマ）＝仏法。仏陀の教え。

Edo（エド）＝江戸。徳川将軍が支配した日本の軍事的首都。1868年の明治維新に東京と改名された。

Futon（フトン）＝布団。伝統的な寝具。昼間に使わないときには丸めて押し入れに収納される。

Gaijin（ガイジン）＝外人。〔日本に来て住む外国籍の人の呼称〕

Go（ゴ）＝囲碁。相対する二人が行う遊戯で、碁盤上で広く地をとったほうが勝ちとなるチェスに似た戦略的ゲーム。

Hato basu（はとバス）＝東京都内の観光バスサービス。

Hirata-gumo（ヒラタグモ）＝平蜘蛛。人家などで普通に見られる蜘蛛。獲物を家屋に運んで食べて、食べ残したものを家に貼りつける習性がある。

Hokusai, Katsushika（カツシカ・ホクサイ）＝葛飾北斎。著名な浮世絵師。生没年（1760－1849）。北斎の最高傑作として『神奈川沖浪裏』（「富嶽三十六景」の一つ）がある。北斎は様々な雅号を使ったが、晩年は好んで「画狂人」を使った。

Irasshaimase（イラッシャイマセ）＝お店やレストランに入ってくる顧客に呼びかける歓迎の言葉、「ようこそ」。

Jin（ジン）＝人、あるいは人々のこと。

Jizo（ジゾウ）＝地蔵（菩薩）。日本の街角のそこここに見られる石像。子供を失った悲しみを持つ親が、地蔵に赤いよだれかけ（エプロン）をかけて、あの世でその子が仏陀に守られますようにと祈る。

Jun ken po（ジュンケンポ）＝子どもの手遊び、「じゃんけんぽん」のこと。

Kago（カゴ）＝（中国、インドの）かご、乗り物。

Kano Motonobu（カノウ・モトノブ）＝狩野元信（1476-1559）。室町時代の日本画家。「阪之下」〔現在亀山市、鈴鹿峠を超えた東海道の宿場町〕の美しさを描こうと努力を重ねたが、満足のいく仕事ができずに筆を谷に投げ込んだ。坂ノ下の風景はあまりに美しく、描くことができない画家泣かせの場所と知られている。〔筆捨嶺〕

Kameyama（カメヤマ）＝日本の天皇、第90代亀山天皇。在位期間1259-1274〔三重県北部の東海道の宿場町、石川氏の城下町〕

Kanji（カンジ）＝漢字。日本のアルファベット（表意文字）で、中国の象形文字を基にして作られた。

Kimono（キモノ）＝着物。男女ともに着用する伝統的な日本の長着。両見頃を左前（右見頃の上に左見頃を重ねる）にして体に巻きつけ、「帯」と呼ばれるベルトで固定する。例外は死者を葬る時で、この逆（右前）となる。

Kyoto（キョウト）＝京都。794-1868までの日本の首都。

Maiko（マイコ）＝舞妓・舞子。芸妓（芸者）見習いの少女。

Mansion（マンション）＝現代的なアパート・マンション。出入りの安全が保障されている多層建築物。

Michi ni mayotte shimaimashita（ミチニ・マヨッテ・シマイマシタ）＝「私は道に迷ってしまいました」

Mudra（ムドゥラー）＝仏陀の印、印相〔梵語〕。手指をもって作る種々の形。右手を胸まであげて、親指と人差し指をつけて手のひらを外に向ける施無畏印。「恐れるなかれ」（恐怖心を取り除くこと）を意味する。

Namu Amida Butsu（ナムアミダブツ）＝南無阿弥陀仏。仏教の称名。「私は阿弥陀仏（無量光仏）に帰依する」の意。〔阿弥陀仏は念仏によって極楽往生を説く浄土宗、浄土真宗で本尊とされる。〕

Nihonbashi（ニホンバシ）＝日本橋。東京（江戸）の中央区（中心）にある橋で、東海道五拾三次の出発点であり、日本各地への距離が計られる起点となる場所。
Nori（ノリ）＝海苔。食用の海草。

Nyubai（ニュウバイ）＝入梅・梅雨の始まり。

Obasan（オバサン）＝おばさん。原義は祖母のことだが、年配の女性に愛情をこめて使う言葉。〔原義は祖母のことと説明されているので、「おばあさん」を意味していると思われる。年配の女性は、「おばさん（叔母、伯母）」から発生した呼び名。〕
Oden（オデン）＝おでん。冬に食べる料理で、かつおの出汁で作ったスープストックにゆで卵、魚の練り物、大根などを入れて煮たもの。

Onryo（オンリョウ）＝怨霊。恋人から受けた仕打ちに恨みを抱いて現世に戻り、男に祟りをする女の死霊。〔一般的には、怨霊は女に限らない。〕

Sakura（サクラ）＝桜の木〔日本の国花〕

Sanjusangendo（サンジュウサンゲンドウ）＝三十三間堂。京都の東山にある寺院で、千一体の（千手）観音像で有名〔正式名称は、蓮華王院本堂〕

Shibori（シボリ）＝日本の絞り染。布を糸で固く縛って折り曲げたり捻ったりして染める染色方法。「嵐」あるいは「嵐しぼり」は、嵐の時の雨脚のように斜めのデザインを施した絞りをいう。

Soba（ソバ）＝蕎麦。そば粉を原料とした日本の細麺。食べ方には、海苔をかけたざるそばや汁そばがある。

Tabi（タビ）＝足袋。親指のところで別れたソックス。

Tanuki（タヌキ）＝日本の狸。昔話などに、身を隠したり人を化かす動物としてよく登場する。のろまでぼんやりした動物で、陶製のタヌキは庭の置物としてよく見受けられる。

Tatami（タタミ）＝畳。い草や藁で作った日本の伝統的床敷き。

Tengu（テング）＝天狗。日本の昔話に出てくる伝承上の生き物で、鳥の頭部と人間の体を持つ。

Tennin（テンニン）＝天人。女性は「天女」と呼ばれ、西洋の天使や妖精に似た日本仏教の天上界（霊的な）の存在。この世に二人といないような美しい女性で、えも言われぬ色彩の衣をまとっている。「天人」は「羽衣」と呼ばれる羽でできた着物をつけて空を飛ぶことができる。

Tojimbo cliffs（トウジンボウ断崖）＝東尋坊。京都の北、福井県の沿岸にある断崖の景勝地。自殺の名所。

Tokaido（トウカイドウ）＝東海道。江戸から京都に至る主要な街道。〔江戸時代の五街道の一つ〕

Tokonoma（トコノマ）＝床の間。日本の和室にしつらえた一段高くなった小空間。掛け軸や花が飾られる。

Torii（トリイ）＝鳥居。神道の神社に通じる門。

Townsend Harris（タウンゼント・ハリス）＝（1804−78）日本に最初のアメリカ領事館を開設した。将軍に謁見するために三島まで東海道を下った。

Ukiyo（ウキヨ）＝浮き世、憂き世。「浮世絵」とは、定めのない儚い世（浮世）を描いた絵を意味する。

Washi（ワシ）＝和紙。伝統的な手法で作られた日本の紙。

Yamabushi Tengu（ヤマブシ テング）＝山伏天狗。山野にすむ悪鬼や小鬼で、動物や人間に変身する力があり、人の夢に入ってきて唇を動かさずに話をする。

Yoisho（ヨイショ）＝英語の「ヒーヴ・ホー」（もちあげろ、よいと巻け）に似た掛け声、間投詞。

コラム参考文献

安村敏信・岩崎均史　『広重と歩こう東海道五十三次』小学館　2000
浦上敏朗「間違い探し　広重画」『芸術新潮』新潮社　1993年3月号
亀山美術館『歌川広重　保永堂版　東海道五拾三次』　2010
五街道ウォーク・八木牧夫　『ちゃんと歩ける東海道五十三次　東』山と渓谷社　2014
五街道ウォーク・八木牧夫　『ちゃんと歩ける東海道五十三次　西』山と渓谷社　2014
児玉幸多監修『東海道五十三次　広重から現代まで』第一法規 1985
鈴木重三・木村八重子・大久保純一『保永堂版　広重 東海道五拾三次』岩波書店　2004
町田市立国際版画美術館（監修）・佐々木守俊　『歌川広重保永堂版 東海道五拾三次（謎解き浮世絵叢書）』二玄社　2010

歌川広重の「東海道五拾三次」と *Tokaido Road*
－青の往還－

岡野 智子

1．歌川広重について
2．保永堂版「東海道五拾三次」の成り立ち
3．広重の「東海道五拾三次」の魅力
4．「東海道五拾三次」と *Tokaido Road*

　歌川広重（寛政9年〜安政5年、1797〜1858）が手掛けた浮世絵版画「東海道五拾三次之内」（保永堂版、以下「東海道五拾三次」と略記）。東海道を宿場ごとに取り上げ、その景観を描いた全55枚からなるシリーズは天保4年（1833）頃出版された。この作品は、当時数え年37歳（以下年齢は数え年）の広重はもとより、浮世絵版画界においても、それらを享受した江戸時代後期の人々にとっても画期的な作品となった。美しく、時にユニークな画風は多くの支持を得て、出版後180年余りを経た今もなお、人々を魅了してやまない。
　ナンシー・ガフィールド博士もその一人で、1977年にアメリカのオレゴンで初めてこの版画を目にした時の印象が、34年を経て詩集 *Tokaido Road* に結実した（その経緯は 6 Totsuka の冒頭に記されている）。ここでは *Tokaido Road* のインスピレーションの元となった広重の「東海道五拾三次」について概略を記すとともに、版画と詩の接点を二つの点から述べる。

1．歌川広重について

　歌川広重は寛政9年（1797）、幕府の定火消同心、安藤源右衛門の長男として、江戸八代洲（八重洲）河岸に生誕した。他の浮世絵師と異なり武家の出身であることが特筆される。文化6年（1809）13歳の時、父の隠居に伴い定火消職を継いだ。職務の傍ら、15歳の時に当時人気の浮世絵師歌川豊広の門人となり、翌年には歌川広重を名乗っている。20代の前半は役者絵・武者絵などを主に手掛け、24歳頃からは美人画にも腕を揮うようになった。27歳の時、家職を養子仲次郎に譲ったが、その後も後見人として34、5歳頃まで同心職にあったとされる。現代に例えれば、広重は東京消防庁に勤めながら、人気のアニメ工房にも所属して絵を描いていたような前半生であったといえよう。
　30代半ばにさしかかった広重に転機が訪れる。主力の画題を次第に役者絵や美人画から名所絵へと転換。37歳の時、「東海道五拾三次」を出版し、絶大な人気を得て以降風景版画のシリーズ（揃物）を最も得意とするようになる。天保7年（1836）、40歳の時には「木曾海道六拾九次之内」、最晩年には120枚セット（目録と二代広重作の1枚を含む）の「名所江戸百景」シリーズなどいずれも浮世絵風景版画を代表する名作を次々と描いた。安政5年（1858）、江戸で流行していたコレラにより9月6日、62歳の生涯を閉じた。

2．保永堂版「東海道五拾三次」の成り立ち

　「東海道五拾三次」は、天保4年から翌5年正月にかけて出版された。当初鶴屋喜右衛

門の仙鶴堂と竹内孫八の保永堂の共同出版で始まったが、中途から保永堂の単独出版となった。広重は後に多くの「東海道もの」を手掛けているので、この「東海道五拾三次」は特に「保永堂版東海道五拾三次」と呼ばれている。

このシリーズは53の宿場に加え、起点の日本橋と終点の京都を入れ、全55図から成る揃物。東海道の風景を横大判の錦絵で描いた最初の浮世絵版画である。初摺が好評を博したため、天保5年（1834）には全図を中折にして貼り合わせた画帖の体裁で再版された（後摺）。その後も重版を重ねたようで、初摺と後摺で異なる表現も随所に見受けられる。

広重の「東海道五拾三次」が大ヒットした背景には、18世紀末頃に起こった旅行ブームに伴い、1800年代の始めにかけて、「東海道」をめぐる多くの出版物が発行されたことが挙げられる。よく知られるところでは、秋里籬島の『東海道名所図会』（寛政9年、1797）、十返舎一九の滑稽本『東海道中膝栗毛』（享和2～文化11年、1802～14）などがあり、浮世絵では葛飾北斎（1760～1849）が東海道の揃物を既に7種も描いていた（1801～14）。

一方一般の絵画界でも、名所図や山水図、実景図が多く手掛けられるようになり、谷文晁の『日本名山図会』（文化元年、1804）など、出版物を通して各地の地形や名所風俗などが関心の的となった。

こうした動きに加え、天保元年（1830）には伊勢への御蔭参りが流行、庶民の間でも街道を行き来する旅が楽しまれるようになる。

さらに特記すべきことは、「東海道五拾三次」刊行の前年、天保3年（1832）に北斎が「冨嶽三十六景」を発表したことである。北斎は当時大量に輸入された青系の化学顔料（通称ベロ藍＝ベルリンブルーの略称）を積極的に用いて、濃い青を基調とした画風を打ち出し、独創的に富士を描いて高い賞賛を得た。それまでの北斎の名所絵は主に人物表現に力点がおかれていたが、「冨嶽三十六景」においては大胆な構図や視点を取り入れ、迫力に満ちた風景版画の世界を切り開いたのである。

こうした浮世絵風景版画の新たな展開を背景に、仙鶴堂と保永堂というふたつの版元から大きな期待を託されたのが広重であった。

3．広重の「東海道五拾三次」の魅力

広重の「東海道五拾三次」の大きな魅力は、各図に漂う豊かな抒情性、情感に冨む景趣といえよう。朝霞や夕映えの空。霧や夕闇に浮かぶ宿場。朝に夕に移りかわる日の光や翳り、大気の湿り気までも広重は巧みに捉えている。

風景だけでなく、街道を行き交う旅人の姿も広重は濃やかに描いた。月明りの中を歩む親子（13沼津）、吹きすさぶ風の中、橋の上で佇む男（44四日市）。街道の傍らで干瓢作りに精を出す母子の姿（52水口）など、印象的な人物の配置は鑑賞者の共感を呼んだだろう。16蒲原では、雪の降りしきる宿場を行く旅人が、モノトーンを基調とした雪景色の中に描かれる。蒲原(静岡県静岡市)の地は本来滅多に雪が降らず、描かれた光景は言わば「絵空言」である。しかし広重は、イマジネーションを駆使して「雪中の旅人」というモチーフをシリーズ中に挿入したのである。

同様に46庄野（三重県鈴鹿市）は、激しい雨の中を急ぎ足で行く駕籠や旅人が描かれる。墨の濃淡のシルエットで表わされた竹林、画面を斜めに横切る街道、逆方向からの斜線による驟雨が幾重にも重なり合い、シリーズ中最も複雑で動きに富んだ名場面となっている。庄野の辺りも実は穏やかな平地で、街道周辺にこうした地形は見当たらない。本図もまた、広重の独創的な場面構成と位置づけられるだろう。

橋や木、船などのモチーフを大きく画面手前に配する構図は、後に広重が「名所江戸百景」

などで積極的に活用し、後年ヨーロッパでゴッホなど印象派の画家たちが大きな影響を受けたことが知られる。その萌芽も「東海道五拾三次」に見出され（7 藤澤、27 掛川、29 見附、30 浜松、32 荒井、42 宮、43 桑名など）、以前の名所絵よりも効果的な構図が起用されている。

一方で穏やかな旅の情景を描いた場面も多く見出され、広重が一図を発行するごとに、緩急をつけて鑑賞者を楽しませた様子がうかがえる。55 図がどのようなペースで随時発売されたか定かではないが、発行の都度それを手に取った江戸の庶民の話題となり、次の刊行が心待ちにされたことと想像される。

広重は「東海道五拾三次」において、一日のうちの光の変化や天象を、ぼかしや陰影を巧みに組み合わせ、名所の景趣を詩情豊かに演出した。さらに意表を突く構図を時に織り交ぜて「揃物」を楽しむ鑑賞者の期待に応えた。旅という非日常への憧れをかきたてつつ、日常的な光景も挿入し、親近感溢れる画面を構築していったのである。

4.「東海道五拾三次」と *Tokaido Road*

さて *Tokaido Road* は広重の「東海道五拾三次」をベースにしながらも、必ずしも版画の内容と詩とは一致をみない。その乖離の狭間に読者である我々がたゆたう余地があるのだが、敢えて版画と詩の接点を挙げるなら、*Tokaido Road* の諸編における blue 又は indigo への言及に注目したい。

北斎の「冨嶽三十六景」ほどではないが、「東海道五拾三次」もベロ藍をほとんどの版画に使用しており、海、川などの水景はもとより空、雲、地平、山影、屋根、藍染めの着物などに鮮やかな青色（藍色）を施している。言わば青（藍）は「東海道五拾三次」においても基調となる色と言って過言ではない。

6 Totsuka において、ガフィールド博士は初めて「東海道五拾三次」を見た時の印象をThe first of these are indigo but gradually monochrome evolves into brocade.（始めそれらは藍であったが次第にモノクロームから錦に展開する）と述べている。この藍（青）のイメージは詩においても随所に用いられ、*Tokaido Road* を象徴する色彩となっている。オペラに再編された際も、舞台の照明が多く blue を基調としていることが極めて印象的であった。

何より詩人は最後の詩、55 Kyoto の最終のスタンザをこう締めくくっている。

I let you go, my blue familiars, cross the bridge alone.	さあ　行きなさい　わたしの 蒼く親しきものたちよ　橋を渡りなさい その身ひとつで　（池田訳）

東海道五十三次の旅は京都三条大橋を渡って終わる。55 編の詩を読んできた読者の旅もこれで幕を閉じるのだが、道連れであった読者を blue familiars と表現しているのではないか。blue が広重と詩人を繋ぎ、読者の旅路の基調でもあったことを示唆しているように思われる。

最後に「東海道五拾三次」と *Tokaido Road* のさらなる往還について触れておきたい。22 岡部（静岡県岡部町）は暗い山中の道を描く場面だが、詩には iris や maple branch and vine が登場する。実は版画の岡部の副題は「宇津之山」。『伊勢物語』第 9 段「東下り」中の「宇津の山」の地で、物語では業平一行が、蔦や楓が生い茂る暗い山道で心細い思いをする場面である。そしてその前には燕子花(iris)が咲く三河国八橋（やつはし）の場面があった。

この「八橋」「宇津の山」（「蔦の細道」ともいう）の二場面は、『伊勢物語』の中でも最も知られた部分で、絵画や工芸意匠にも多く描かれてきた。広重はもちろん、江戸の人々

は「宇津の山」といえばそうした『伊勢物語』の情景やキーワードを連想したはずである。

　ところが版画では敢えてそれらを想起させるようなモチーフは描かれていない。にも拘わらず、詩において、場面のキーワードである「燕子花」「蔦楓」が登場することに私は強い関心を抱いた。ガフィールド博士に伺ったところでは、22 Okabe において『伊勢物語』は全く念頭になかった由だが、そうであればなおのこと、平安時代の物語・江戸の版画・現代の英詩が期せずして共鳴したことになる。

　日本の美術は古来、和歌や俳句と多く接点を持ち、共通のイメージをさまざまな手法で表わしていった。歌（詩）を楽しみ絵に憩う。絵に遊び歌（詩）に誘う。両者の出会いと往還が、今、英詩の世界を得て、我々を新たな豊穣の旅へと導いている。

Hiroshige Utagawa's *Fifty-Three Stations of the Tōkaidō* and *Tokaido Road*
A Dialogue in Blue

Tomoko Okano

1. Hiroshige Utagawa
2. The Hōeidō edition of the *Fifty-Three Stations of the Tōkaidō*
3. The Appeal of Hiroshige's *Fifty-Three Stations of the Tōkaidō*
4. *Fifty-Three Stations of the Tōkaidō* and *Tokaido Road*

The Hōeidō edition of the *Tōkaidō gojū santsugi no uchi* or *Fifty-Three Stations of the Tōkaidō* by Hiroshige Utagawa (1797-1858) is a series of fifty-five ukiyo-e prints which depict all the stations on the Tōkaidō road. It was published in 1833. This work was ground-breaking not only for Hiroshige, who was then about thirty-seven years old, but also for the world of ukiyo-e prints and the people of the later Edo Period who appreciated them. Hiroshige's beautiful and unique artistic style continues to attract viewers to this day, more than 180 years later.

Dr. Nancy Gaffield is one such viewer. Her first impressions upon seeing Hiroshige's work in 1977 in Oregon were articulated thirty-four years later in her collection of poetry titled *Tokaido Road*. (These circumstances are explained at the beginning of the poem *6 Totsuka*.) This essay offers a brief overview of Hiroshige's *Fifty-Three Stations of the Tōkaidō*, her source of inspiration for *Tokaido Road*, and explores two points of connection between the prints and the poetry.

1 Hiroshige Utagawa

Hiroshige Utagawa was born in Yayosu (Yaesu) Gashi in Edo (today's Tokyo) in 1797, the first son of Gen'emon Andō, a firefighter under the Edo Shogunate. It is noteworthy that Hiroshige was born into a samurai household unlike other ukiyo-e artists. When he was thirteen years old in 1809, Hiroshige succeeded his father as a firefighter when the latter retired. While working as a firefighter, he apprenticed himself at the age of fifteen to the famous ukiyo-e artist Toyohiro Utagawa and was given the name Hiroshige Utagawa the following year. Hiroshige mainly produced *yakushae* (portraits of kabuki actors) and *mushae* (portraits of warriors) in his early twenties, and began *bijinga* (portraits of beautiful women) when he was about twenty-four years old. At the age of twenty-seven, he passed on the headship of the family to his adopted son Nakajirō, and as Nakajirō's guardian, continued the same occupation until the age of thirty-four or five. A present-day analogy would be as if Hiroshige spent the first half of his life drawing at a famous animation studio while working at the Tokyo Fire Department.

The turning point for Hiroshige was when he was in his mid-thirties. The main subject of his art shifted from *yakushae* and *bijinga* to *meishoe* (pictures of famous places). After publishing the *Fifty-Three Stations of the Tōkaidō* at the age of thirty-seven, Hiroshige gained tremendous popularity. From then on his skill was most evident in his sets of landscape prints. Hiroshige produced one masterpiece after another, including ukiyo-e prints of landscapes such as the *Sixty-Nine Stations of the Kiso* in 1836 at the age of forty and *One Hundred Famous Views of Edo* at the end of his life. On the sixth day of the ninth month in1858 he passed away at the age of sixty-two due to an outbreak of cholera in Edo.

2　The Hōeidō edition of the *Fifty-Three Stations of the Tōkaidō*

The *Fifty-Three Stations of the Tōkaidō* was published between 1833 and New Year's Day in 1834. At first, it was published jointly by Kiemon Tsuruya of Senkakudō and Magohachi Takenouchi of Hōeidō, and later independently by Hōeidō. As Hiroshige created many prints categorized as *Tōkaidō mono* (*Tōkaidō* prints), this early publication of the *Fifty-Three Stations of the Tōkaidō* is specifically called *The Hōeidō edition of Fifty-Three Stations of the Tōkaidō*.

The series is of fifty-five prints including the starting point at Nihonbashi, Edo, and the end point in Kyoto and all the fifty-three stations on the Tōkaidō. It was the first large-size *nishikie* (full color) woodblock print series depicting landscapes of the Tōkaidō. As the first print run, (*shozuri*) was favorably received, in 1834 the entire series was reprinted (*atozuri*) in the form of a *gajō* (picture album) with a central binding. It seems that this series was printed many times, as there are many differences between the first print and the reprints.

Hiroshige's *Fifty-Three Stations of the Tōkaidō* gained great popularity in part because many books on the Tōkaidō were published in the early 1800s as a result of the travel boom at the end of the eighteenth century. A few well-known examples are *Tōkaidō meisho zue* (*Pictures of famous places along the Tōkaidō*) by Ritō Akisato (1797), the humorous novel *Tōkaidōchū Hizakurige or Shank's Pony along the Tōkaidō* by Ikku Juppensha (1802-14). As for ukiyo-e prints, Hokusai Katsushika (1760-1849) had already produced as many as seven different sets of prints of the Tōkaidō (1801-14).

Meanwhile in the painting world, *meishozu* (paintings of famous places), *sansuizu* (paintings of landscapes), and *jikkeizu* (paintings of actual landscapes) began to be produced in great quantities, and through publications such as the *Nihon meizan zue* or *Pictures of Noted Mountains* by Bunchō Tani (1804), geographical features of places, famous places, and customs became the subject of viewers' interest.

In addition, *okage mairi* (group pilgrimages to Ise Jingū) became fashionable in 1830, and ordinary people began to enjoy their journey on this highway.

One further point of significance is that in 1832, the year prior to the publication of the *Fifty-Three Stations of the Tōkaidō*, Hokusai produced the *Thirty-Six Views of Mount Fuji*. He liberally used Prussian blue chemical pigment commonly called Berlin blue (*bero-ai*), which was imported in large quantities then, and he established an art style which used the dark blue pigment. His unique paintings of Mt. Fuji using the blue pigment were greatly admired. While Hokusai used to place emphasis on the depiction of figures in his paintings of famous places, in the *Thirty-Six Views of Mount Fuji* he adopted bold compositions and viewpoints and paved the way to a new world of powerful woodblock prints of landscapes.

Thus, considering the circumstances of these new developments in the art of the landscape print, the two publishers Senkakudō and Hōeidō held high expectations that Hiroshige would produce excellent work.

3 The Appeal of Hiroshige's *Fifty-Three Stations of the Tōkaidō*

Some of the most appealing aspects of Hiroshige's *Fifty-Three Stations of the Tōkaidō* are the rich lyricism found in each print and the emotions filling every scene. Hiroshige skillfully captured atmospheric conditions such as mist in the morning and the glow of the evening sky, an inn in the fog and at dusk, and changes in light - the bright morning sunlight and the diminishing sunlight in the evening, he even captured the dampness of the air.

Hiroshige finely depicted not only scenes but also travelers passing on the highway. For instance, in *13 Numazu* a parent and child walk in the moonlight, in *44 Yokkaichi* a man stands on the bridge in the gusty wind, and in *51 Minakuchi* a mother and child work hard at making *kanpyō* (dried gourd shavings) at the side of the road. The impressive compositions of these figures must have evoked viewers' empathy. A monochrome snow scene in which travelers pass by an inn is depicted in 16 Kambara. In fact, it rarely snows in Kambara (Shizuoka City) thus, the depicted scene is in a way a fantasy. However, Hiroshige efficiently used his imagination and embedded the motif of travelers in the snow in the series.

Similarly, *46 Shōno* (Suzuka-City, Mie Prefecture) depicts palanquin bearers and travelers hurrying along in heavy rain. The scene consists of a bamboo grove painted in silhouette against a background of ink gradation, a road obliquely crosses the scene, and the strong rain is illustrated with diagonal lines in the opposite direction. This tremendous scene is full of movement and compositionally, the most complex one in the series. The area of Shōno, in fact, is flat land, and none of the geographical features depicted in the scene are found near the Tōkaidō. This print can thus be understood as Hiroshige's unique composition.

Hiroshige's other compositional devices included setting objects such as a bridge, timber, and a ship in the foreground and are seen in *One Hundred Famous Views of Edo*. This kind of composition eventually had a major impact on impressionist painters in Europe such as Vincent Van Gogh. It's origin can be found in the *Fifty-Three Stations of the Tōkaidō* in *7 Fujisawa, 27 Kakegawa, 29 Mitsuke, 30 Hamamatsu, 32 Arai, 42 Miya,* and *43 Kuwana* in which more dynamic compositions are used compared to earlier prints of famous landscapes.

On the other hand, many scenes depicting the peaceful sights of the journey are also found, which suggests that every time Hiroshige published a new print, he made changes for viewers to appreciate. The timing of the release of all the fifty-five prints is not certain, but it can be imagined that upon every publication, each print must have become a topic of conversation among the common people of Edo, and they must have looked forward to the next publication.

Hiroshige produced prints of famous places full of poetic sentiment by expressing changes of light and weather during the day, skillfully combining gradation and shadow. Furthermore, he sometimes included a composition which would surprise viewers, and which responded to their expectations. In short, Hiroshige established a style stimulating the common people's longing for the extraordinary to be found on a journey, while bringing familiarity to the viewers by adding scenes of ordinary life.

4 *Fifty-Three Stations of the Tōkaidō* and *Tokaido Road*

Tokaido Road was inspired by Hiroshige's *Fifty-Three Stations of the Tōkaidō*, and yet, it does not necessarily correspond with the contents of the prints. This divergence between the two provides readers a free imaginative space. That being said, if we are to find a particular connection between the poems and the prints, we should pay attention to the references to blue or indigo in some poems of *Tokaido Road*.

Prussian blue is not used as heavily as in Hokusai's *Thirty-Six Views of Mount Fuji*, but Hiroshige used it for almost every print of the *Fifty-Three Stations of the Tōkaidō*. These prints have vivid blue not only for scenes of water such as the sea or a river but also for the sky, clouds, the horizon, a shadowed mountain, roofs, and a kimono dyed with indigo. In other words, it is no exaggeration to say that blue is the basic color for the *Fifty-Three Stations of the Tōkaidō*.

In *6 Totsuka*, Gaffield stated her impression when she saw the *Fifty-Three Stations of the Tōkaidō* for the first time: "The first of these are indigo but gradually monochrome evolves into brocade." Her image of indigo (blue) is used for many of the poems, and it functions as the symbolic color of *Tokaido Road*. When this collection of poems was made into an opera, blue was used for most of the stage lighting and left a strong impression.

Importantly, the poet concludes the final stanza of *55 Kyoto* as follows:

> I let you go, my blue
> familiars, cross the bridge
> alone.

The journey through the fifty-three stations of the Tokaido ends after crossing Kyoto Sanjō Ōhashi Bridge. The journey of the readers who have been reading the fifty-five poems also comes to an end here. Would it not be the case that the poet refers to the readers, fellow travelers, as "blue familiars"? It seems to me that the poet suggests that blue provides the connection between Hiroshige and the poet and functions as the key to the readers' journey.

Lastly, let us explore one further connection between the *Fifty-Three Stations of the Tōkaidō* and the *Tokaido Road*. The print *22 Okabe* (Okabe, Shizuoka Prefecture) is a scene depicting a path in the dark forest, whereas the poem *22 Okabe* mentions iris, maple branches, and vines. In fact, the subtitle of the print is *Utsunoyama Mountain*. This is the same place as Utsunoyama, which appears in *Azuma kudari* (*Going down to the Eastern Provinces*) in episode 9 of *Ise Monogatari* or the *Tales of Ise*, where Narihira and his party fearfully cross the dark mountain path full of thick ivies and maples. Additionally, the scene before this is Yatsuhashi of Mikawa Province where irises bloom.

These two scenes, Yatsuhashi and Utsunoyama, also called *Tsuta no hosomichi* or *Narrow Ivy Road*, are the most well known scenes in the *Tales of Ise*. They have been depicted in many paintings and crafts. Hiroshige as well as the people of Edo would have naturally imagined the scenes and recognized the key words of the *Tales of Ise*. However, Hiroshige did not intentionally depict motifs associated with the *Tales of Ise*. On the other hand, this author's interest was caught by the fact that the poem *22 Okabe* contains keywords such as iris, ivy and maple. When asked about it, Dr. Gaffield said she did not think about the *Tales of Ise* when writing *22 Okabe*. If that is the case, this resonance between the tales of the Heian Period, the prints of the Edo Period, and contemporary English poetry is all the more unexpected.

From olden times, Japanese visual arts have had many contacts with the poetry of waka and haiku and expressed common images in various ways. We enjoy the poems and appreciate the paintings; we find pleasure in the paintings and are drawn into the poems. With this encounter we enjoy the interaction of the world of English poetry and Japanese prints, which leads us to new and fruitful journeys.

二つの東海道
― 英詩『東海道ロード』と東西の邂逅 ―

池田 久代

はじめに ― 浮世絵と旅を謳う文学
1. 視覚芸術と詩歌の結婚 ― エクフレイシス
2. 詩型 ― 詩のスタイルと主題
3. 二つの東海道 ― 時空を超えた円環の旅

はじめに ― 浮世絵と旅を謳う文学

　もう6年半ほど前になる。英国のカンタベリー市にあるケント大学のダーウイン・カレッジで激務にあったナンシー・ガフィールド博士を訪ねたのは、アーモンドの花木やスミレ、水仙が美しく咲き始める3月の末のことだった。日本ではあの東日本大地震と福島原子力発電所の津波被害に国中が騒然としていたちょうどその時だった。

　ガフィールド博士が、長年の日本への憧れを一冊の詩集にまとめて、処女詩集『東海道ロード』（Tokaido Road、2011）を上梓したのはちょうどこの年であった。アメリカ生まれで英国在住のこの大学教員は、本作品でアルデブラ・ファースト・コレクション賞（ロンドン）を受賞し、以後、詩人としてのもう一つの顔を持つことになる。

　歌川広重の風景版画（浮世絵）は19世紀より西欧の画家たちを様々に魅了してきたが、西欧にあって初めて「広重の眼」を獲得したのは、アメリカの画家・版画家のジェームス・M・ホイッスラー（James M. Whistler、1834−1903）であった。（Noguchi・3）風景の全体像をその細部まで捉え、限りなく描写しようとする「西洋の眼」にとって、浮世絵の空間造形力や視点のユニークさは驚くべき発見であった。広重の「風景」を見る眼は、自然が見せる表情の瞬間的様相を斬新に切り取る。その分離（孤立）の瞬間に自然が見せる稀有な個性、孤独のうちに立ち現れた世界が、広重の集中と暗示性の芸術である。（Noguchi・5）

　詩集『東海道ロード』において、ナンシー・ガフィールドはこの「広重の眼」を現代詩というメディアを通して表現している。広重の東海道と現代アメリカ詩の幸運なる出逢いと、両者のなかに秘められた声、暗示的・多音声的情感の交錯が、この作品の醍醐味と言える。叙情的・予言的・革新的な広重の「東海道」が呼び覚ましたこの「詩の旅」は、東西二つの文化の架け橋となるだろう。

1. 視覚芸術と詩歌の結婚 ― エクフレイシス

　詩集『東海道ロード』は、若き日の詩人と歌川広重の浮世絵版画『東海道五拾三次』（1833）との晴天の霹靂のごとき邂逅に端を発している。この詩集は、広重に倣って江戸の日本橋から京都の三条大橋まで55の短詩が連ねられている。ここに編まれた詩集は、しかしながら、今や世界的に名を轟かせている広重の『東海道五拾三次』の浮世絵を、その視覚芸術を、西洋人の眼で単に言語化（文学化）した説明詩ではない。

　詩人は述べている。「詩を書くとは、対話を封印することではなく、開くこと」。詩とは、他の芸術作品、作り手、読者に開いていく行為だ。（講演録・34）それは版画と詩の間に

想像上のつながりを作り出す行為であり、詩人は広重の旅に同行しながら、「空想の世界にある人物、景色、愛しい人々、日本への思い出を詩の中に投影し、「どこでもない世界」（空・無の世界）を生み出したかった」、と述べている。（同上・37）

　この詩集では、ホメロスの『イリアス』に語源を持つ、美術作品に対応した詩作法＝「文学的エクフレイシス（ekphrasis）」＊が実践されている。（同上・34）ちょうど、英国詩の父であるジェフリー・チョーサー（Geoffrey Chaucer、1340−1400）が、ボッカチオの『デカメロン（十日物語）』の枠組みを使って、ロンドンからカンタベリーへの巡礼の旅『カンタベリー物語』（24編の物語詩）を書いたように、『東海道五拾三次』という視覚芸術は、詩人が自己の実在（リアリティ）と物語を一体化させるための「装置」、詩人の言葉を借りれば、「借景」の役目を果たしている。『東海道ロード』は、広重の借景を飛びだして、非現実の時空の中で、あるいは、現実と幻の間でたゆたう生のリアリティを刻んだスリリングな現代詩である。広重の『東海道五拾三次』は、詩人が自らの内なる「異界」を覗き込むための窓と言えるかもしれない。

2. 詩型 — 詩のスタイルと主題

　本詩集の詩型はバラエティに富んでいる。各詩の連（スタンザ）は、英詩の伝統を踏まえた二行連句・対句（カプレット・couplet）、三行連句（ターセット・tercet）、最も一般的な四行連句（クオートレイン・quatrain）など、形態的には古典的なスタンザ数を組み合わせて構成されているが、音の数や文字数に一定のパターンがなく、古典的な韻も踏まない自由詩（フリー・ヴァース）となっている。連の組み方（数）と詩的イメージの間には何らかの関連性があるように思われる。詩行の視覚的構成や余白が、語られた言葉（内容）と連動して、読者をさらに深い共感へと導く。詩型の中で最も多用されているのは二行連句（カプレット）で、55詩のうちで9詩に及んでいる。（7, 9, 12, 13, 16, 19, 36, 50, 53）例えば、第16宿の雪の「蒲原」は、広重の『東海道五拾三次』の版画のうちでも名作中の名作であるが、同タイトルの英詩は、9連のカプレットの軽妙なテンポとリズムの中に、画狂老人と女の狂気が対峙され、迫力のある詩人の想像力が躍如し、版画に勝るとも劣らない力を与えている。

　また、東西の数にまつわるイメージを並置した散文詩「39 岡崎」や、松尾芭蕉の『奥の細道』の「俳文」を思わせる散文から始まる自伝的散文詩「6 戸塚」、また版画の場所から喚起された日本の故事や伝説などを謳いあげたエピソード詩なども秀逸な抒情詩と言えるだろう。「9 大磯」の虎ガ雨、「19 江尻」の羽衣伝説、「26 日坂」の小夜の中山の夜泣き石伝説など、説明を極力剥ぎ取った短くシャープな音の連鎖がものの哀れを呼び起こす。詩人の胸に去来する愛憎、悲哀、親子愛が、風景の中に溶け込んで波紋のように広がっていく。

　さてこの詩集には、4人の人物が登場する。広重を思わせる芸術家のヒロ、その恋人のマリコ（茶の師匠）とキクヨ（旅の芸者）、そして一人称の語り手「わたし」は、ある時は「川」になり、ある時には「詩人の影」となって、フーガ（遁走曲）のように絡み合い、時空を超えながら旅を続ける。

　『東海道五拾三次』の版画を借景として、人物たちの様々な心象風景が、虫や鳥の声、雨の音、吹きすさぶ風、深々と降り積もる雪、八月の月、椿、菊、夾竹桃などの花（花鳥風月の風景）によって織りなされる。そしてその叙情豊かなイメージの背後に、「川（自然の試練）」があり、「街道（人の道）」がある。過酷な運命を強いる自然の猛威、人の世の嘆きの川を越えて、旅人は京師・三条大橋にたどり着く。旅立ちから到着への「旅」、生から死への「旅」、死から来世への「旅」、情念から静謐への「旅」、そして「立斎広重

死絵」の偈(「東路に筆を残して旅の空　西のみ国の名ところを見ん」)にあるような、仏教的諦観(悟り)を求める西方浄土への「旅」は、果たしてこの詩の旅の終焉に垣間見えたのか。今は、そしてつねに、私たちは終わりなき旅の「途中」を歩き続けているのかもしれない。円環の旅は果てしなく続いていく。

　もう少し、詩を覗いてみよう。

　版画「46 庄野」は、「蒲原」と並び称される広重の東海道の名作である。しかし、広重が描いた山坂は今はなく、平坦な田野が続いている。版画では、白雨(夕立)に出会って坂道を行き交う農夫と旅の籠、見知らぬ者同士のすれ違い、広重の好んだ旅の本質(出逢いと別れ)が描かれている。墨絵のような風景の美しさの中に、詩人はイチイの木の不気味さ(西欧では墓場に植えられる木)、死へと疾走する人間たちの末路を見ている。人間の営為を静かに見つめる雨に煙る竹やぶや古木こそがこの詩の主人公なのかもしれない。

　「22 岡部」の詩もまた、広重が描いた「蔦の細道」(宇津の谷峠)のイメージと見事に呼応している(『伊勢物語』の九段の舞台、「在原業平の東下り」となった古道)。高みに菖蒲の花が咲き、楓と蔦が生い茂る峠道の侘しさ、寂しさは、恋しい男を追いかけてここまでやってきた女の内奥の悲嘆と呼応するが、女のあてのない焦燥に応えるのは、森のツグミの声ばかり。日本文学に永遠に残ったこの蔦の細道のイメージ「駿河なる宇津の山辺の現にも夢にも人に逢わぬなりけり」は、ガフィールドの詩によってもうひとつの生命を与えられ、千年の昔男の愛惜が切々と蘇る。

　さて、版画「7 藤沢」は、前面にそそり立つ大きな鳥居に仕切られるように時宗総本山の清浄光寺(遊行寺)と江ノ島弁財天への参道が配された版画であるが、この詩は広重の版画世界とは一見無関係に、「アッシュベリーの『詩とは何か』を読んで」という枕詞から始まっている。日本の読者にはいかにも唐突な詩の始まりだ。「詩とは何か」という詩は1970年代から顕著になってきたジョン・アッシュベリー(John Ashbery、1927−2017)の新しい表現形式・詩論の表明詩で、ある瞬間に偶然に聞こえた会話や出来事を詩の中に投入する詩作法だ。それも詩人の実体験に基づいている—ある朝ニューヨークのエンパイヤーステイトビルで偶然に出会った名古屋から来たボーイスカウトの少年たちに出会ったことである。「それは中世の町で、そこには名古屋から来た／ボーイスカウトの装飾帯がある?」(The medieval town, with frieze/ Of boy scouts from Nagoya?)(飯野・99)「藤沢」詩ではカプレットの最終連が「稀有なる個の本質は　孤独のうちに出現する・・・」と結ばれる。これは江ノ島弁財天の女神たちに対峙した詩人の覚醒体験と言えるかもしれない。女の胎内、孤独なる洞窟の中に、広重が出現した。ヨネ・ノグチの広重の風景画論がこの詩の中で受肉している(Hiroshige・4-7)。

　アッシュベリーをはじめとする現代アメリカ詩の背後には、1970年代以降にアメリカが受けた日本・禅ブームの影も見受けられる。「偶然性」の詩は、デザイン(意図)を捨ててチャンス(偶然)に身を委ねることにより、主客の分断のない全的な世界を模索した。アッシュベリーは1950年代にコロンビア大学で鈴木大拙の禅の講義を聞いて、仏教の「空、融通無碍」の世界観、西洋合理主義を脱した偶然性、今ここの実在性を模索した詩人だ。ガフィールドの東海道詩においても、随所にブッダ(仏陀)を求める詩人の声が響いている。

3. 二つの東海道 — 時空を超えた円環の旅

　人は何かを求めて旅立ち、そしてどこかに終着する。歌川広重は1833年に江戸から京都へ向かう浮世絵『真景・東海道五拾三次続画』の旅を終えた。ナンシー・ガフィールドは1970年代にアメリカから飛び立ち、2011年に広重の東海道の詩の旅を終えた。

人は誰もそれぞれの旅立ちとそれぞれの旅の終焉を走り抜ける。ある時は恋しい人を追いかけて、またある時は、肉親の愛を求めて、失った子を探し、人の世の定め（諦観）を模索し、永遠のやすらぎの地（西方浄土・天国）を求める。ガフィールドの『東海道ロード』はさまざまな旅のかけがえのなさ、悲しみ、静寂、美しさをありありと私たちの目前に立ち昇らせてくれる。この詩集は、私たちに、超えるべき人生の山坂を叙情豊かに呈示する。出発から到着への「旅」、生まれては死んでいく「旅」、そして、出発と到着の間を、果てしなく繰り返す円環の旅の諸相が語られる。

　『東海道ロード』の詩の旅は、一つの挑戦であったと言えるかもしれない。昭和の初期に日欧を往復した国際派詩人ヨネ・ノグチ（Yone Noguchi、1875-1947）は、広重の風景画を論じて、西洋は「広重の眼」を獲得したと述べた。「こうして、西洋に発見されてこの方、広重は明らかに新しい理解によって解釈され、再構築された。西欧人にとって、広重は一つの発見であり創造物となった。並々ならぬほどに」。(Noguchi・13 拙訳) 西欧の眼をもったヨネ・ノグチは、広重の「死絵」の偈は、当時のよくある人生の結辞（辞世）ではなく、英語に翻訳されるともう一つの強烈なメッセージを伝えてくると述べた。広重の「東海道」は、江戸期の日本、現代の日本にとどまらず、西欧に向けて開かれて行く広大な旅の始まりであったのかもしれない。その証左が、ナンシー・ガフィールドの『東海道ロード』として結実している。「東海道」の旅は今後も、様々に続いていくだろう。

注：
＊エクフレイシスとは、ギリシア語の「エク」＝外へ向けて、「フレイシス」＝語りかける）の合成語で、詩人は、エクフレイシスの概念を説明するために、W.H. オーデンの有名な詩「美術館」を例にとって、自らの詩作の特質を説明している。この作品は、一方では広重の版画シリーズの宿場名に従って展開した「現実的・特定型のエクフレイシス」を基盤にしながらも、詩が浮世絵から抜け出して、想像の世界に飛翔していく「観念的・超現実型のエクフレイシス」となっている。（講演録・36）

参考文献：
飯野友幸『ジョン・アッシュベリー「可能性への賛歌」の詩』、研究社、2005.
坂野康隆『広重の予言』、講談社、2011.
ナンシー ガフィールド「詩と旅」（講演録）『比較文化から見た日英文学・教育講演会』
　　皇學館大学津田学術振興基金プロジェクト編、2013.
Yone Noguchi, 'Hiroshige', 'Hiroshige and Japanese Landscapes', In *Books on Ukiyoe and Japanese Arts in English by Yone Noguchi, Series: Collected English Works of Yone Noguchi,* Vol.1)), edited by Shigemi Inaga, Edition Synapse, 1921, pp.1-32, 1934, pp.8-77.
Helen Vendler, *The Breaking of Style: Hopkins, Heaney, Graham.*
　　Harvard University Press, Cambridge, Massachusetts, London,
　　England, 1995.

Two *Tōkaidōs*
Tokaido Road and the Encounter between East and West

Hisayo Ikeda

Introduction: A Journey of *Ukiyo-e* and Literature
　1.　The Marriage between Visual Arts and Poetry: Ekphrasis
　2.　Poetic Form: Styles and Themes
　3.　Two *Tōkaidōs*: a Cyclical Journey beyond Time and Space

Introduction: A Journey of *Ukiyo-e* and Literature

　It was six-and-a-half years ago that the author visited Dr. Nancy Gaffield at Darwin College, Kent University, Canterbury, England. It was the end of March 2011, the almond trees were in blossom, and violets and narcissus flowered. That month Japan faced the turmoil of the Great East Japan earthquake and tsunami which crippled the Fukushima nuclear power plant and claimed thousands of lives. Dr. Gaffield published *Tokaido Road* that year. It was her first collection of poetry and it was an expression of her long-lasting love for Japan. A university faculty member, Dr. Gaffield, an American currently living in England, received the Aldeburgh First Collection Prize for Poetry for this collection. Since then, she has held a second career as a poet.

　Hiroshige Utagawa's woodblock prints of landscapes (*ukiyo-e*) have been attracting western artists in various ways since the nineteenth century. It was the American artist, James M. Whistler (1834-1903) who understood "Hiroshige's eye" for the first time in the West (Noguchi: 3). At that time Western artists endeavored to capture the entire picture of a landscape in detail and depict it completely, so it was a remarkable discovery for them to see the capacity of ukiyo-e to create such a space with its unique perspective. Hiroshige's eye for landscape uniquely grasps the momentary phase revealed in nature. The particularity that nature unveils at the moment of isolation, and the world which appears in that isolation is the art of Hiroshige's concentration and subtlety (Noguchi: 5).

　In *Tokaido Road* (2011) Gaffield expresses "Hiroshige's eye" through the medium of modern poetry. It can be said that the real fascination of this work is the fortunate encounter between Hiroshige's *Fifty-Three Stations of the Tōkaidō* and contemporary American poetry embodying the interplay of the hidden voice and suggestive multi-faceted emotions. This poetic journey, inspired by Hiroshige's *Tōkaidō* with its lyrical, prophetic, and innovative nature, will become a bridge between Eastern and Western cultures.

1 The Marriage between Visual Arts and Poetry: Ekphrasis

Tokaido Road originates with the totally unexpected encounter of the young poet with Hiroshige's woodblock prints *Fifty-Three Stations of the Tōkaidō* (1833). *Tokaido Road* consists of fifty-five poems, following Hiroshige's journey from Nihonbashi of Edo (present day Tokyo) to Sanjō Ōhashi of Kyoto. However, the poems are not mere verbal renditions of Hiroshige's globally renowned prints or a commentary on their visual artistry from a Westerner's perspective.

The poet states: "The writing of poems is not meant to be an act of containment, but an act of opening the dialogue…with other works of art and their makers, and importantly, with the reader, too" (Gaffield: 45). It is also an act of fostering imaginative links between the prints and poetry. According to Gaffield, while paralleling Hiroshige's journey along the Tōkaidō, she "projected imaginary characters, scenes, personal preoccupations, and memories from the time she lived in Japan to create what Buddhists call 'nowhere land'" (Gaffield: 47).

In the collection, literary ekphrasis* is employed. This is a method of writing a poem related to a work of art and is derived from Homer's *Iliad* (Gaffield: 45). In the same way as Geoffrey Chaucer (1340-1400) used the structure of Giovanni Boccaccio's *Decameron*, when he wrote about the pilgrimage from London to Canterbury in *The Canterbury Tales*, the visual art of the *Fifty-Three Stations of the Tōkaidō* plays the role of a device in order to unite the poet's own reality with the story, or in the poet's words, the "borrowed scenery." *Tokaido Road* is thrilling contemporary poetry that goes beyond the borrowed scenery of Hiroshige and depicts the reality of life oscillating in an imaginary time and space or between reality and illusion. It can be said that Hiroshige's *Fifty-Three Stations of the Tōkaidō* is the window through which the poet looks into 'another world' within herself.

2 Poetic Form: Styles and Themes

Tokaido Road employs a variety of poetic forms. The stanzas of each poem consist of classic combinations based on the tradition of English poetry- the couplet, tercet and the most commonly seen quatrains and others. However, the poems have no particular pattern in terms of the number of syllables and words, and they are free verse without classical rhyme. The stanzas and poetic images are in pertinent combinations. So that the visual structure of a line of verse line and the space links to the narrative and leads the reader to a deeper empathy with the content. Among verse forms, it is the couplet that is most often used, and nine among fifty-five poems employ it (Numbers 7,9,12,13,16,19,36,50, and 53). For example, *16 Kambara* is a masterpiece among Hiroshige's prints. In the poem of the same title, the uplifting tempo and rhythm of nine verses of couplets express the confrontation between the madness of the old artist and that of a woman, and the poem vividly manifests the poet's imagination and is as powerful as the print.

There are also some excellent lyrical poems such as *39 Okazaki*, a prose poem in which parallels between Japanese and Egyptian ceremonial occasions are shown through numerical correlations; *6 Tozuka*, an autobiographic-style prose poem which starts with a piece of haiku style prose recalling Matsuo Bashō's *Oku no hosomichi* (*The Narrow Road through the Provinces to the Deep North*). In addition are poems narrating Japanese historical events and legends associated with the places of the prints such as *Tora ga ame* (*Toragozen's Rain*) in *9 Ōiso*; *Hagoromo densetsu* (a legend of a heavenly maiden's robe of feathers) in *19 Ejiri* and *Sayo no Nakayama yonaki ishi densetsu* (a narrative of a big stone crying at night at the pass) in *26 Nissaka*. In this poem a chain of short, sharp sounds inspire *mono no aware*, the pathos of things, as the result of paring down the narrative to a bare minimum. Emotions recurring in the poet's heart such as love and hatred, sorrow, and love between a parent and a child dissolve into the scene and spread out like ripples.

Tokaido Road features four characters: Hiro, the artist Hiroshige, the two women he loved named Mariko, a tea master, and Kikuyo, a geisha on a journey, and "I" the narrator expressed in the first person. "I" becomes a river at times and the poet's shadow at other times, entwining together in a fugue-like sequence, and continuing to travel beyond time and space. Using the images of *Fifty-Three Stations of the Tōkaidō* as borrowed scenery, the characters' emotional worlds are expressed through *kachōfūgetsu* or flower-bird-wind-moon combinations of natural phenomena such as the voices of insects and birds, the sound of rain, blowing wind, falling snow, the August moon, camellias, chrysanthemums, and oleander. The image of the river, which can be understood as the hardships of nature and the image of the road, the path of life, lie behind the lyrical images. After surviving the fury of nature that compels human beings to confront their harsh fate and the river of lamenting in this world, the travellers finally arrive at Sanjō Ōhashi Bridge in Kyoto. At the end of this poetic journey we may ask: Have the travellers glimpsed the journey from departure to arrival, the journey from birth to death, the journey from death to the afterlife, and the journey from emotion to tranquility? Have they glimpsed the journey toward the Western Pure Land where they will find Buddhist enlightenment as expressed in Hiroshige's death poem on his *shinie* (the woodblock print issued after his death). He wrote "I depart on a journey, leaving my brush in the East, and hope to see the wonderful places in the West." Now and forever we continue to walk the endless journey. The cyclical journey goes on without end.

Let us look at a few more poems. Hiroshige's print *46 Shōno* is a masterpiece of the *Tōkaidō* series, however the mountain path he depicts is very different from the flat rice fields we see there today. In the print peasants and palanquin-bearers are caught in a heavy shower. Strangers passing each other on the road evoke Hiroshige's favorite theme of the essence of the journey: namely meeting and parting. The poet watches human beings running at full speed toward death, through the beauty of scenery reminiscent of an ink painting and the eeriness of the yews (which are planted in graveyards in the West). Perhaps the bamboo grove and old trees are the main subjects of this poem, quietly watching the humans run their course.

22 Okabe also excellently responds to the image of *Tsuta no hosomich* , also known as *Utsu no tanitōge, Narrow Ivy Road*. This is the ancient road known as *Ariwara Narihira no Azuma kudari* (*Ariwara no Narihira's Journey to the East*) in episode 9 of *Ise Monogatari* (*Tales of Ise*). The desolation and loneliness of the road over a mountain pass where irises bloom on the heights, and the maples and ivy that grow thickly respond to the inner grief of a woman who has followed her lover over the pass. Yet the only response to her hopeless restlessness is the sound of forest thrushes. The image of the narrow ivy road expressed in the *Ariwara no Narihira* poem has a permanent place in Japanese literature: "On the mountain slopes of Utsu in Suruga, neither awake nor in my dreams can I meet with my beloved that I so long to see." Gaffields's poem gives further life to this image and ardently revives the man's love of a thousand years ago.

7 Fujisawa depicts the large *torii* gateway standing so tall in the composition that it cuts across the path leading to Shōjōkōji Temple (also called Yugyōji), the head temple of the Buddhist Time Sect, Jishū, and Enoshima Benzaiten Shrine. In contrast, Gaffield's poem begins with: "*After Ashbery's 'What Is Poetry'*" which seems to be unrelated at first glance to the world of Hiroshige's print. To Japanese readers, the start of the poem is indeed surprising. *What Is Poetry* is a poem by John Ashbery (1927- 2017) in which he suggested a new style of expression and theory of poetry that he prominently promoted from the 1970s. His poetry makes use of conversations accidentally heard and events which happen randomly. He illustrates this in a personal experience. One morning, he coincidentally encountered boy scouts from Nagoya at the Empire State Building in New York: "The medieval town, with frieze / Of boy scouts from Nagoya?" (Iino: 99). The second line of the final verse of the couplet in Gaffield's poem *Fujisawa* concludes with "The rare individual nature reveals in isolation…." It can be said that this line is the poet's experience of enlightenment upon encountering the goddesses of Enoshima Benzaiten Shrine. Hiroshige emerges in a womb or isolated cave. We are reminded of Noguchi's analysis that Hiroshige's art manifests in isolation and concentration. (Noguchi: 4-7)

The influence of Japanese culture and Zen Buddhism, which experienced a boom in American society after 1970s, can be found behind American contemporary poetry such as Ashbery's. He rejected Western rationalism and centered on the nature of accident by discarding design or intention and instead entrusting to chance and coincidence. He sought the world of entirety where the separation of subject and object does not exist. Ashbery went to Daisetsu Suzuki's lectures on Zen at Columbia University in the 1950s. He sought the Buddhist world view of *kū*, emptiness, and *yūzūmuge*, being unfettered and flexible, as well as exploring the nature of accident and the reality of the here and now. In Gaffield's *Tokaido Road*, the poet's voice seeking Buddha resonates here and there.

3 Two *Tōkaidōs*: a Cyclical Journey beyond Time and Space

We leave on a journey seeking something and eventually arrive somewhere. In 1833, Hiroshige Utagawa finished his journey of *Fifty-Three Stations of the Tōkaidō*. Similarly, Gaffield departed America in the 1970s and completed her poetical journey of Hiroshige's *Tōkaidō* in 2011.

Anyone may go on a journey and run through to its end while following a lover, seeking affection of their family, searching for a departed child, exploring the state of mind detached from the world, or pursuing the land of eternal peace (the Western Pure Land or a heaven). Gaffield's *Tokaido Road* vividly reveals the uniqueness, sorrow, silence, and beauty of various kinds of journey. The poetry lyrically shows us the mountain road of life that we need to overcome. The poetry narrates a journey from departure to arrival, from birth to death. Various aspects of the journey of the cycle between the departure and the arrival repeat without end.

It can be said that the journey of the poems in *Tokaido Road* is a challenge. The internationally-minded Japanese poet Yone Noguchi, who traveled back and forth between Europe and Japan during the early Shōwa period, discussed Hiroshige's landscape prints and stated that the West had gained Hiroshige's eye: "Thus Hiroshige, since being discovered in the West, was interpreted and reconstructed by a decidedly new understanding; so he is to a certain great degree, a discovery or creation of Westerners" (Noguchi: 13). Noguchi, who acquired a Western eye, stated that Hiroshige's death poem on his *shinie* can be understood in a conventional way by Japanese, but it conveys a more intense message when translated into English. It might be the case that Hiroshige's *Tōkaidō* is not just limited to Edo and contemporary Japan but is the beginning of a great journey opening to the West. One outstanding example is Nancy Gaffield's *Tokaido Road*. The journey of *Tōkaidō* will continue in various ways in the future.

Note
* Ekphrasis is a compound word made up of 'ek' meaning out and 'phrasis' meaning speaking. Taking W.H. Auden's famous poem *Musée des Beaux Arts* as an example, Gaffield explains the concept of ekphrasis and her method of writing the poems of *Tokaido Road*. Her work falls into ekphrasis of the actual closed type which means it is based on the names of the post towns of Hiroshige's prints, but it is also notional ekphrasis of the conceptual kind as her poems go beyond the prints and fly into the world of imagination (Gaffield: 45-47).

References
Iino, Tomoyuki. *John Ashbery: Kanōsei eno sanka no shi*. Tokyo: Kenkyūsha, 2005.

Sakano, Yasutaka. *Hiroshige no yogen*. Tokyo: Kōdansha, 2011.

Gaffield, Nancy. *The Poem and the Journey: From Tokaido Road to a Poetics of Place* in Kento Daigaku, Kogakkan Daigaku gakujyutsu koryu shinpojiumu, Ise City: . Kogakkan University Tsuda Gakujutsu Shinkō Kikin Project, 2013.

Noguchi, Yone. *Hiroshige, Hiroshige and Japanese Landscapes* in *Books on Ukiyo-e and Japanese Arts in English* ; in the series *Collected English Works of Yone Noguchi*, Vol.1, edited by Shigemi Inaga. Tokyo: Edition Synapse, 1921, pp.1-32, 1934, pp.8-77.

Vendler, Helen. *The Breaking of Style: Hopkins, Heaney, Graham.* London: Harvard University Press, 1995.

訳者あとがきと謝辞

池田 久代

　本詩集『東海道ロード』は *Tokaido Road*, London, CB editions, 2011 の全訳です。日英両言語（原詩と翻訳）を併記した本書の出版は、皇學館大学津田学術振興基金の助成により、足掛け3年の研究会活動の成果として、実現の運びとなりました。また本書の出版は、著者であるケント大学文学部（School of English）のナンシー・ガフィールド博士の『東海道五拾三次』という版画作品や日本文化への熱い想いに支えられて実現したことは言うに及びません。

　本書には多くの方々から有形無形の協力をいただきました。かめやま美術館（三重県亀山市）の小倉昌行館長のご厚意により、同館所蔵の保永堂版『東海道五拾三次』を使わせていただきました。付録の朗読 DVD には、詩人自身によるポエトリー・リーディングを収め、そのバックグラウンドには、本学事務方の斎藤愛美・敏ご夫妻のご協力で、中村洋一氏作曲の『組曲・東海道五十三次』（尺八・三絃・箏・十七絃の四重奏の五十五の宿場の完全収録版、2014年）を使わせていただきました。中村洋一氏は、国内はもとより、ベルギー、フランスなどの海外公演で自作を披露されています。この組曲は、広重の『東海道五拾三次』との出会いに感動して、1968年から2011年までの半世紀をかけて作曲・演奏されてきたものです。さらに、表紙の装丁の一部として、国際的視野で墨・象世界を追求しておられる墨書家の吉田礼子氏より、題字の寄贈をいただきました。これらの有難い協力によって本書にかつてないユニークな趣が添えられたことは、編者一同、望外の喜びです。

　英語による日英文化の比較研究と発信というプロジェクトに、最後まで精力的に関わってくださった伊勢市民の方々（三村健、中村則子、林農、大西昌子、水野逸夫様など）、皇学館大学の教員、学部生、大学院生など、研究会参加者の皆様に心よりお礼を申し上げます。

　江戸美術・浮世絵の専門的立場から、研究会で広重の版画の解説を引き受けてくださった岡野智子氏（京都・細見美術館上級学芸員）のご協力と、解題（「歌川広重の「東海道五拾三次」と *Tokaido Road*」）の執筆に心よりお礼を申し上げます。

　さらに、仕上がった翻訳原稿の校正の労をとってくださった玉木ダーナ氏（米国メイン州在住の日系二世、元同志社女子大学教員）にお礼を申し上げます。

　最後になりましたが、本書の制作編集に関わったプロジェクトチームを紹介します。広重の東海道版画の解説コラム、まえがき、DVD 編集は児玉玲子（第二期プロジェクトチーフ）、詩の朗読の原音録音はクリストファー・メイヨー（第三期・現プロジェクトチーフ）、そして、全詩の翻訳、解題（「二つの東海道―英詩『東海道ロード』と東西の邂逅―」は池田久代（第一期プロジェクトチーフ）が担当しました。

　この詩集は、広重の『東海道五拾三次』の版画を見たことがない西欧の読者にとっても、詩が内包するポエジー（詩情）が強力に喚起される秀逸な現代詩です。訳詩にあたっては、詩の行数を原文に合わせ、原詩の短く歯切れのよいハードボイルドな美しさや寂寥感、言葉の明晰さやリズムを削ぎ取らないように努めました。

　しかしながら、「翻訳とはつねに叛逆であり、せいぜい金襴の裏地に過ぎない」（岡倉天心『茶の本』）。詩の翻訳に至っては何をか云わんや、です。不可能への挑戦、不遜な試みでしたが、原詩と版画を併記して拙い邦訳を補い、二つの文化を繋ぐ架け橋を築こうと努めました。読者の皆様のご理解と忌憚のないご教示をお願いいたします。

著者紹介

ナンシー・ガフィールド （ Nancy Gaffield ）

アメリカ合衆国生まれ。1979 年から 5 年間日本に住む。現在英国ケント州のカンベリーに在住。英米現代詩、詩学を専門とする学者であり詩人。
ケント大学文学部（スクール・オブ・イングリッシュ）の上級講師（博士）としてクリエイティブ・ライティングを教える。2017 年退職。

Tokaido Road『東海道ロード』（2011）は処女詩集で、2012 年にアルデブラ・ファースト・コレクション賞を受賞。その他に 5 冊の詩集がある。*Owhere*（2012）テンプラー・パンフレット賞受賞、*Continental Drift*（2014）、*Zyxt*（2015）、*Meridian*（2016）、*Tokaido Road* のオペラ台本 *Tokaido Road: A Journey after Hiroshige*（2014）出版。

訳者紹介

池田 久代（Hisayo Ikeda）

山口県生まれ。
同志社女子大学 大学院文学研究科修士課程修了。奈良女子大学 大学院人間文化研究科比較文化学博士課程満期退学。米国ハーヴァード大学 英語・英文学部客員研究員（2007-2009）。皇學館大学教授を定年退職（2015）

著書：（単・共・編著）
『天心・岡倉覚三とアメリカーポストモダンをみすえてー』（2015）、『堀至徳日記』（2016）（以上、皇學館大学出版部）、『岡倉天心―伝統と革新』（大東文化大学東洋研究所 2014）、『長谷寺所蔵　岡倉天心書簡』（茨城大学五浦美術文化研究所 2011）、『もっと知りたいニュージーランド』（弘文堂 1997）、『ニュージーランド百科事典』（春風社 2007）、『ニュージーランドを知るための 63 章』（明石書店 2008）など。

翻訳書：（単著）
ティク·ナット·ハン著『微笑みを生きる』（1995）、『生けるブッダ、生けるキリスト』（1996, 2017）、『禅への道』（2005）、『小説 ブッダ いにしえの道、白い雲』（2008）、『死もなく、怖れもなく』（2011）、『〈気づき〉の奇跡』（2014）、『イエスとブッダ』（2016）、スティーヴン・A・ミチェル著『愛の精神分析』（2004、以上春秋社）など。

執筆、編集者紹介

池田　久代　（Hisayo Ikeda）
　皇学館大学元教授、現在皇學館大学非常勤講師
　奈良女子大学大学院人間文化研究科博士後期課程単位取得満期退学
　研究分野：英米文学、日欧比較文学

児玉　玲子　（Reiko Kodama）
　皇学館大学文学部コミュニケション学科教授
　名古屋大学大学院文学研究科博士後期課程単位取得満期退学
　研究分野：英語学、英語カリキュラム開発

クリストファー・メイヨー　（Christopher Mayo）
　皇学館大学文学部コミュニケション学科准教授
　米国プリンストン大学大学院東洋学部修士課程修了
　東洋学博士
　研究分野：歴史学

岡野　智子　（Tomoko Okano）
　細見美術館上席研究員、皇學館大学非常勤講師
　学習院大学文学部人文科学研究科博士後期課程中途退学
　研究分野：日本美術史

東海道ロード

平成30年10月20日発行

発 行 所　皇學館大学出版部
代 表 者　山 口　建 史
　　　〒516-8555 伊勢市神田久志本町1704
　　　TEL 0596-22-6320

印 刷 所　株式会社オリエンタル
　　　〒510-0304 三重県津市河芸町上野 2100
　　　TEL 059-245-3111

ISBN-978-4-87644-210-2 C3898
本体価格 3,970円＋税